IMPOSTER

IMPOSTER

Cait Levin

Text copyright © 2025 by Cait Levin
Jacket illustrations copyright © 2025 by Oriol Vidal

Code on page 51: Reproduced with permission from Girls Who Code. Girls Who Code Girls 2022, website and platform, accessed 15 March 2024, www.girlswhocodegirls.com.

All rights reserved, including the right of reproduction in whole or in part in any form. Charlesbridge and colophon are registered trademarks of Charlesbridge Publishing, Inc.

At publication, all URLs in this book were accurate. Charlesbridge, the author, and the illustrator are not responsible for the content of any website.

Published by Charlesbridge Teen, an imprint of Charlesbridge Publishing
9 Galen Street, Watertown, MA 02472 • www.charlesbridgeteen.com

Library of Congress Cataloging-in-Publication Data
Names: Levin, Cait, author.
Title: Imposter / Cait Levin.
Description: Watertown, MA: Charlesbridge Teen, 2025. | Audience: Ages 12 and up. | Audience: Grades 7–9. | Summary: "When high school sophomore Cameron Goldberg finally gets the chance to take a computer science elective and then join the competitive RoboSub team, she must learn how to battle her imposter syndrome and let her talents shine."—Provided by publisher.
Identifiers: LCCN 2024012462 (print) | LCCN 2024012463 (ebook) | ISBN 9781623545635 (hardcover) | ISBN 9781632894410 (ebook)
Subjects: LCSH: Women in computer science—Juvenile fiction. | Sex discrimination against women—Juvenile fiction. | Impostor phenomenon—Juvenile fiction. | Teenagers—Juvenile fiction. | Self-confidence—Juvenile fiction. | Parent and child—Juvenile fiction. | CYAC: Sexism—Fiction. | Self-confidence—Fiction. | High schools—Fiction. | Schools—Fiction. | Parent and child—Fiction.
Classification: LCC PZ7.1.L48647 Im 2025 (print) | LCC PZ7.1.L48647 (ebook) | DDC 813.6 [Fic]—dc23/eng/20240404
LC record available at https://lccn.loc.gov/2024012462
LC ebook record available at https://lccn.loc.gov/2024012463

Printed in China • OPIC
(hc) 10 9 8 7 6 5 4 3 2 1

Jacket illustration done in digital media
Text type set in Addington
Edited by Karen Boss
Designed by Diane M. Earley
Production supervised by Mira Kennedy

For Claire, who was my Viv.

This book would've been better with your notes.

imposter syndrome *noun*

doubts about your abilities or accomplishments along with fears about people thinking you're a fraud despite evidence of your ongoing success

```
(function imposter(){
    console.log("Chapter");
    console.log("One");
})();
```

Chapter One

Cameron worried she might damage the NFC chip, but it was time to find out. A fan hummed in her open window, ready to exhaust the reek of acetone. It was January in Ohio, but her closed bedroom door meant Cam's parents wouldn't notice the cold. At least not right away.

Cam gripped the tweezers, a Hanukkah gift from her mom. ("It's time to get the hedges in check, nena.") Cam had damaged the antenna when removing her school ID from the acetone jar last time. Not today. She moved the chemically melted plastic aside, exposing the near field communication chip. The thin wire wove away from it. Slowly freeing the wire from the remains of her melted ID, Cam extracted her prize. First hurdle passed.

A knock on her door. And a voice. "Nena, are you coming down for the movie?"

Cam whipped around. "Yes, Mom! I'll be down in a sec."

"Your father has the popcorn ready."

"Okay! I'll be down soon!"

Soft footsteps retreated. Now to coil the antenna and solder it in place on the chip. If Cam messed this up, the signal wouldn't work and the whole thing would be a loss—again.

Cam lit a Hanukkah candle she'd snagged from the box in storage. (Her mother would wonder why there was one missing, but that was future Cam's problem.) She didn't own a soldering iron, but she'd watched a video about how to use an open flame. Plunging the candle into a mini muffin, she picked up her NFC chip.

The candle started to drip. Cam melted the solder she'd snatched from the design lab at school before break. As the solder became malleable, she secured the coil in place. Done.

After the movie she'd use Mom's LED nail dryer to set the device into an acrylic mold. Hopefully the ID ring would be ready to wear back to school tomorrow morning.

Cam heard another "Nena!" from the living room. She blew out the candle, shut off the fan, and ran for the stairs.

‹ br ›

After the movie Dad wanted to chat about the new semester.

"Are you excited for your first elective?" he asked.

"Yeah, I think so." Cam had signed up for the Introduction to Computer Science course. As a sophomore she didn't have a lot of opportunities to take electives. The options were limited: computer science, picking up an extra art, an introductory finance class, or something called FACE (Family and Consumer Education), involving taking care of an animatronic baby. Cam's choice was easy. Being alone in the class made her a bit nervous. (Her best friend, Vivian, had chosen Pottery and Sculpture.) And because it was an elective, there would be juniors and seniors too.

"Are we done with the cocadas?" Mom asked.

Some people thought Cam's parents were a mismatch—Panamanian mother, American father, both Jewish. This was the fateful story of Walt Goldberg and Gabriela Lucía Friedman Rodriguez: met at NYU, discovered their grandfathers served together in Panama during World War II, shared faith. "A Jewish man with ties to Panama," her mother loved to say. "I just knew he was made for me!" Cam's father sold insurance, her mother real estate. And along came Cameron Goldberg, a hybrid in every sense with her mother's olive skin and her father's frizzy, loose curls. A humid day in summer—forget about it!

"What will you do with the coding class? Website design?" Cam's mother asked, clearing away the cookies.

"Maybe. Mostly I just want to know more, so I can figure out what's possible." Cam had always liked to build things. Some of her earliest memories were of helping Dad assemble some new piece of furniture or an appliance. She loved digging through his tools to find just the right one, then putting all the pieces together to make something that would help her family. She still remembered building an oscillating fan for their living room when she was little. That moment of plugging it in, flipping it on, seeing it work—magic.

Recently she'd been watching a lot of different makers on YouTube, Twitch, and TikTok, and there were so many ways to create things. The NFC ring to replace her school ID was her first experiment with wearable technology. Fabrication always felt natural to her, but she'd never really tried to code before. The class was an opportunity to learn more and see if it was for her.

"Well, I think it's fantastic," Dad said. He was always her biggest cheerleader. "You're going to do great. At anything you set your mind to."

"Thanks, Dad," she replied, trying not to roll her eyes. She knew she was lucky to have such supportive parents, but sometimes it felt like living in a sitcom or something. "I'm gonna head up to bed. First day back tomorrow and all."

"Night, sweetie," her dad said, giving her a hug.

"Sleep well, nena," Mom said, kissing her head.

Cam's room still smelled strongly of acetone—so much so that she was sure her clothes and hair smelled like it too. She wondered if her parents had noticed and chosen to ignore it. She plugged in the LED nail lamp to complete the final step: hardening the resin. If all went well, she'd be able to wear the ring to school the next day.

< br >

"Hey!" Viv greeted Cam at her locker. "How was your final night of winter break?"

Vivian had been Cam's best friend since sixth grade, when they'd been the only two students to bring their own lunch to school one day and the teacher made them sit apart from the other kids. Something about food allergies (Cam shellfish, Vivian eggs). They'd been inseparable ever since.

"Great. Watched *Ace Ventura* with the fam," Cam said.

"Again?"

"It's a staple."

"Your family is too cute. I couldn't get my parents to watch a movie together if I starred in it." Vivian's parents had been fighting pretty bad for about a year. Viv thought they might separate soon.

"Check this out." Cam flashed her right ring finger. The NFC chip was set into the purple acrylic her mother sometimes used on her nails. It had hardened under the lamp into a perfect little triangle that hid the hardware. To a casual observer, Cam wore a cheap purple ring with a nondescript design on it, like something from a flea market.

"Does it work?" Vivian already knew about the project and the previous failed attempt.

"Let's find out," Cam replied.

They went down the hall to a side door that led out to an adjoining building. The superintendent had gotten spooked after so many school shootings in the news. So they'd installed a security system the previous year that required all students to wear their ID card or have them handy to wave in front of a sensor to unlock doors. Cam knew there must be a better way. She placed her right hand near the sensor and held her breath. A moment later the indicator light turned green, and she heard the door unlock.

"Whoa, you did it!" Viv said. "I want one! You could make these for everyone!"

"Technically it's against the rules," Cam said, smiling broadly at her success. "We're not supposed to tamper with student IDs."

"I mean, it's not like you made a fake one or anything," Viv said as the girls moved through the hallway.

"Yeah, but melting an ID and tearing it apart is probably not the best."

"Well, I think it's awesome, and I want one! I'll pay you for it."

"I'd never ask you to!"

"Can you do one in teal?"

Cam laughed. "I'm not sure my mom has that color."

They entered the Student Services Office and approached the woman at the desk.

"Hi," Cam said, "I need a new ID."

The woman looked at her skeptically. "Didn't you get a new one before break?"

Cam was prepared. "Yeah. I just realized the wallet I keep it in has a big hole, so I guess it kept slipping out. Won't happen again."

The woman still looked skeptical but gave Cam the form to fill out. "It'll be ready by the end of the day."

Cam thanked her, and the girls scurried out.

"When's your Intro to CS class?" Viv asked.

"First period."

"Now! Have fun!"

"I plan to," Cam said as she peeled off into a classroom. "See you later."

There were eight boys in the room. They all stopped talking when she walked in.

"Can we help you find something?" a junior she recognized asked.

"Oh, I'm looking for Intro to CS?" She knew she was in the right place.

"Yeah, that's in this room. You looking for Ms. McNealy?" Ms. McNealy taught sewing later in the day in this same room.

"No," Cam said, her cheeks warming. "I'm in this class."

A couple boys smiled as they turned back to each other.

Mr. Lenox, the computer science teacher, entered the room. "Hi there," he said to Cam. "Can I help you find something?"

It was a new semester, but this was not Cam's first day at this school. Why did they keep asking her questions like this? *I'm not lost.* Standing a bit straighter, she cleared her throat and hoped the boys wouldn't hear it.

"No. I'm in this class. Where should I sit?"

Mr. Lenox looked surprised but gestured around the room. "Anywhere you like. Welcome."

The eight boys were all sitting in the back rows, so Cam slid into a front seat, grateful for the empty space that separated them. Eight pairs of eyes were on her neck.

"Right. Hello, everyone," Mr. Lenox said. "Let's start by getting a sense of who's in the room. Raise your hand if you're familiar with at least three languages?"

Cam was confused. *Isn't this an introductory course?* She knew enough to realize he meant coding languages. Glancing back, she saw three boys had their hands raised.

"Excellent. Two languages?"

Three more hands went up.

"Just one?"

Two more hands.

Mr. Lenox cleared his throat. "And no languages."

Face flushed hot, Cameron raised her hand. "Mr. Lenox, I thought this was an introductory course. Is that not right?"

"It is, yes," he replied. "But so few students take computer science. The registrar often ends up combining all levels into one course." He moved behind the desk and picked up a whiteboard marker. "Generally students have some previous exposure to coding through extracurriculars or personal interests."

This was news. If Cam had known, she would have spent her whole winter break studying instead of perfecting her ring.

"It's all right, Ms. . . ." He glanced at his roster. "Perez?"

She shook her head, trying not to blush again. This happened to her literally all the time.

"I'm Perez," a boy in the back said, waving a hand. "Jamie Perez."

"Oh. So, Ms. . . ." He paused to search the list again.

"Goldberg," she said, putting them both out of their misery.

"Goldberg, excellent. No need to worry. We'll get you up to speed."

Apparently *up to speed* meant having a working knowledge of CSS. He proceeded to spend the next forty minutes filling the whiteboard with acronyms she'd heard of but didn't understand like HTML, XML, and SQL. He didn't explain—just wrote them as he said them, as if that were enough for everyone to keep up. She took notes furiously, in pace and in feeling, ignoring the stares she could feel boring into her from behind.

When the bell rang, Cam bolted into the bathroom and texted Viv. **Horrifying experience. Send help.**

Her phone buzzed immediately. **Where are you? I'll intercept on the way to English.**

They met near the music classrooms. As they walked toward English, Cam filled Vivian in.

"All guys?" Vivian asked. "Like, not a single girl?"

"All guys," Cam replied.

"Are any of them gay? At least there could be that."

"I didn't get that vibe."

"And they just stared when you walked in?"

"Yep. The room went mute. Like they were spending all their energy staring at me."

"What kind of staring? Like hole-in-your-pants staring or everyone-knows-you-wet-your-pants-in-fifth-grade staring?"

"Like came-to-school-naked staring."

"Geez. That's awful."

They slid into desks next to each other as the bell rang. Cam got out a notebook and placed it discreetly at the edge of her desk where Vivian could see.

Maybe I'll drop out of the class, she wrote. *It's only the first day. I bet I can transfer into something else.*

Viv let her eyes slide over the page while keeping her body turned forward. When she finished reading, she whipped out her own notebook.

What! You can't do that. You're interested in this stuff. You've been waiting for this class!

It's just so uncomfortable, Cam wrote back. *I feel totally alone and like everyone else belongs there except me.*

That's not true! You just need time to catch up. You're going to crush it.

When Cam finished reading, she noticed Vivian had her fist in the air and was mouthing *Crush it.*

"Ms. Knix, did you have a question?" Ms. Elroy asked.

"Nope. I'm good," Viv said.

When Ms. Elroy turned back to the board, Viv turned to Cam and put her fist up again. "Crush it!" she whispered.

It was difficult to focus on the short story they were discussing. Cam's brain was still processing first period. She'd been so excited to start CS—an opportunity to learn something that mattered to her. Fabrication was one thing, but she wasn't allowed to use the design lab unless a teacher brought her class there for a project, which her teachers rarely did. She knew the CS course gave her access, and she needed it if she ever hoped to make things on the level she wanted to.

She tried to remember her middle school typing class, which was as close as she could get to computer science then. It seemed to her that the girls did better in general. They'd also all taken woodworking, which consisted mostly of gluing paper outlines to wood and then sawing out an animal. Cam had made a bunny and found the whole thing pointless. She much preferred making things that had purpose.

As a sophomore, she wasn't very aware of electives juniors and seniors took. When she'd scanned the room that morning, she only vaguely recognized the guys there. Why hadn't she interacted more with these people? What were the clubs and activities Mr. Lenox referred to, and why didn't she know about them?

She wasn't nervous about the work, though. She knew she could catch herself up. There were online tutorials for everything, and she could take whole classes on Python and CSS online. What made her nervous was a gut feeling that this opportunity she'd been so excited about wasn't going to be only learning a new thing and applying it. It was going to be more complicated.

She needed to know more, and fast. They weren't using their computers in English or math, so she had to wait until lunch to full-force google.

Flipping open her laptop in the cafeteria, she searched "learn to code" and found some familiar places: Code.org, Scratch. *We used these in middle school*, she recalled. They were geared toward younger kids. Codecademy looked promising, but there were twelve coding languages, and she had no idea where to start. Some courses were free, but others cost money. Google and Apple had resources too, but for teachers. *Maybe Mr. Lenox should check these out*, she thought. There was an ad for something called SheCodes that also looked good, so she bookmarked it for later. It sparked her curiosity, so she changed her search to "women in coding" and found an article with the headline "The Secret History of Women in Coding."

The subtitle read "Computer programming once had much better gender balance than it does today. What went wrong?"

Uh-oh. Cam read the article, which included information about Mary Allen Wilkes and Lady Ada Lovelace and the women who programmed ENIAC and Elsie Shutt. Young mothers coding at night while their babies napped in the hall; women working from home and teaching each other to code in the fifties and sixties. *This is amazing*, she thought.

But then the article went on about how colleges began offering computer science courses, and women didn't sign up. Some professors looked into why, and it turned out the girls got messaging at home that computers were for boys. Cam read a line that made her stomach drop. "At school girls got much the same message: Computers were for boys. Geeky boys who formed computer clubs, at least in part to escape the torments of jock culture, often wound up, whether intentionally or not, reproducing the same exclusionary behavior." That was *exactly* how she'd felt in class—the way those boys looked at her and stopped talking when she entered the room. Excluded.

Opening a new search, she typed in "women excluded from CS." What she found didn't make her feel any better.

"Why More Than Half of Women Leave the Tech Industry" was the first article she came across. Then "There Are Too Few Women in Computer Science and Engineering" and "When Women Stopped Coding." *Shit*, Cam thought to herself. Even Google employees had staged a walkout. "Dozens of Google Employees Say They Were Retaliated Against for Reporting Harassment," another headline read.

It never occurred to Cam that making and coding were male-dominated fields. The makers she followed on Twitter were women: Sophy Wong, Kim Pimmel, Limor Fried.

She read on. In 2023 only 14 percent of engineers were women. *Fourteen percent!* The percentage of women in computer and math jobs had gone down 11 percent in the last twenty years and was now only 26 percent. She learned that when women speak up about mistreatment, their bosses often don't do anything. Sometimes these courageous women even lose their jobs or are hazed by their coworkers until they leave. New words flashed across her screen: *implicit bias, stereotype threat, gaslighting, imposter syndrome.*

She wanted to throw up. She also wanted to throw her computer out the window.

"Are you okay?" Vivian snapped Cam out of her research nightmare.

"Did you know that 87 percent of women working in Silicon Valley have had demeaning comments made to them by male colleagues?" Cam replied.

Vivian paused, holding a potato chip inches from her mouth. "No, I did not know that."

"And 88 percent of those women report that male coworkers won't even make eye contact with them!"

"That's messed up."

Cam leaned back in her chair. "This is madness! Women in tech fields deal with a monumental amount of nonsense on a daily basis!"

Viv gently closed Cam's laptop, a concerned look in her eyes.

Cam rubbed her face, massaged her temples. "Why didn't we know about this?"

Vivian shrugged. "I don't know. Because we live in Ohio?"

"Ugh!" Cam put her head on the table.

"What's the big deal?" Vivian asked.

Cam's head snapped up.

"I mean, obviously this is terrible," Viv went on. "But we already know gender equality is terrible. Remember all that #MeToo stuff?" She pushed a pudding cup closer to Cam.

"This feels different," Cam said, opening the cup and digging in.

"Why?"

Because this is what I want to do, Cam thought. But she just shrugged.

"Listen, if you want more female engineers, then be an engineer!" Viv said. "You always make cool stuff—stuff I could never even think of."

"But the way I felt this morning—the only girl in the room. That's what it's like everywhere—in all the rooms." She gesticulated wildly with her spoon.

"Right. But if *you* hadn't been there, then no girl would've been there."

This wasn't making Cam feel better.

"We talk about this in DECA all the time. If you want things to be different, then get in there and make a difference!"

In general Cam metaphorically rolled her eyes when DECA came up. (Any club about business and marketing that got amped up about cookie sales and blue blazers weirded her out.) But she knew the point Vivian was making was right.

Still, Cam wasn't the type of person who prided herself on making waves. Her main goal was to be invisible enough to avoid gossip *about* her, yet visible enough to stay in the gossip loop. She'd done a pretty good job so far.

"I just don't want to feel like I did this morning every day for the rest of my life."

"You won't!" Vivian countered. "You'll see. This was only day one. Your power will grow over time. Daenerys Targaryen was sold to a horse warlord when we first met her!"

"I'm not sure *Game of Thrones* is the best counterexample for gender-inequality issues."

"I disagree! Listen, it's like Daenerys said: 'I'm not going to stop the wheel. I'm going to break the wheel.' Break the wheel, sister!"

"Are we comparing me to Daenerys *pre* burn-everyone-alive or *post* burn-everyone-alive?"

"Oh, *pre*, definitely *pre*." Vivian popped open a bag of chocolate chip cookies and offered Cam one. "And who knows if that'll happen in the books anyway. That could've been about showing off cool TV graphics."

Or about Daenerys losing her mind after fighting her whole life to be treated like a capable person, Cam thought.

```
(function imposter(){
    console.log("Chapter");
    console.log("Two");
})();
```

Chapter Two

After school Cam and Viv walked over to Aldo's, a pizza and ice cream place where kids hung out. Cam swirled her straw around in her drink, lost in her thoughts about the weird day. Then she realized she hadn't asked Viv about her elective.

"Hey, how was pottery?" she asked.

Viv perked up a little. "Oh, it was great! Ms. Newberry is going to live up to the legend. I can tell. And I finally have access to the artsy-sensitive male demographic I've been searching for."

Cam laughed. Viv had always been boy crazy. "Any interesting prospects?"

Viv shrugged. "Oh, you know, pretty much the same crowd we've known our whole lives, so the pickings are slim as ever. But at least some of those guys have stopped eating their boogers. When they pop on a beanie, they might even get close to a Cole Sprouse vibe if you squint and try to ignore ten years of memories."

Cam shared Viv's frustration—they'd grown up with the same kids their whole lives. Sometimes it felt like they were destined to be single until college. Neither Viv nor Cam had ever had a boyfriend or even a real date. They didn't count the people they had "dated" in middle school, whatever that meant then.

Viv sighed. "Sometimes I'm so tired of being tragically single. Movies and TV have taught me to yearn for more. Where's my geeky sidekick? Someone who I get a new haircut for and fall in love with? Where's my secretly sensitive but perpetually misunderstood football quarterback? The murder we solve solidifies our bond forever?"

"I think you've been watching too much *Riverdale*," Cam said.

Viv huffed. "Maybe everyone else is watching too little."

< br >

That night Cam set the table with her mom while her dad finished making dinner.

"How was your first day back?" Mom asked.

"Oh, you know," Cam said. "New haircuts. New backpacks. Same kids."

"How was your new coding class?" Dad asked, bringing out a roast chicken.

Cam shrugged as she sat down. "It was fine."

"Hmm. Tell us more, nena." Her mom always knew when she was keeping something from them.

"I don't know. It was kind of a weird vibe."

"Weird how?" her dad asked.

"I'm the only girl."

Her parents glanced at each other. "That seems strange," her mother said. "All the sophomores get to take electives this semester, don't they?"

"Uh-huh."

"It could be random," Dad offered. "Maybe it changes year to year."

"The teacher said that not very many people sign up, so they combine the classes."

Her parents gave each other a look Cam knew meant *Maybe we should be worried about this.*

"Were the boys unkind to you?" Mom asked, scooping potatoes onto her plate.

Cam shrugged again. "I don't know. Not really." How could she articulate what it felt like? They hadn't been mean in any obvious way. But they certainly weren't welcoming.

Her mom frowned. "Did the teacher seem good?"

"Maybe?" Cam replied. "He moved really fast. He mostly wrote on the board and lectured. I expected it to be a little more hands on. Like, more interactive." She paused to chew some chicken and then mumbled a bit of truth. "He was surprised to see me when he arrived, like he thought I was in the wrong class."

Her dad's eyebrows shot up. "I'm sure he didn't. That would be . . ."

"Rude," Mom supplied.

Cam nodded. "He asked if I was looking for a different class."

Her parents exchanged another glance. "I can't say I like that for you, nena," her mom said.

"I did some research," Cam said. "Technology and engineering are both male-dominated fields. So if I'm interested in doing this kind of stuff long-term, this might be what it's like."

Her dad leaned back in his chair. "Now that I think about it, all the guys in our IT department are, well, guys."

Mom pursed her lips and made a *tch* sound—an expression of particular annoyance that Cam had come to fear over the years. "Well, so what?" Mom countered. "The class is for everyone, so the teacher should make sure all students feel welcome."

Dad frowned. "What can we do to help?"

"I'm not sure," Cam said. "I got kind of bummed out about the whole industry, really."

A pause. Cam felt her parents doing that thing they sometimes did—having a silent conversation with context she didn't have. They weren't the type to charge into school and ask for change, and Cam wasn't the type to want that. And what would they ask for? *Hey, Mr. Lenox, can you and these boys be a little less annoying?*

"Well, if we're going to talk about women being mistreated, we're going to need chocolate brownies," her mother said, taking their plates as she stood up.

Her father leaned over. "I hope you'll stick with it, Cam," he said. "This was just one day. We're here for you, if you need anything."

"Thanks, Dad."

It did help a little, knowing her parents would support her no matter what. And remembering that it was just the first day. Maybe it was a particularly bad first impression. But still, her radar was turned fully on, and she wouldn't be caught unprepared.

The food coma she went into after two of her mom's legendary brownies helped too.

```
(function imposter(){
    console.log("Chapter");
    console.log("Three");
})();
```

Chapter Three

The next day in class there was yet another boy, bringing the total count up to nine. He was in Cam's grade, and she thought she remembered his name. Jack, maybe? Jackson—that was it. He wore ill-fitting jeans and a dark zip-up hoodie with some kind of art she couldn't identify. He was engrossed in his Alienware laptop.

It felt to Cam like the air sucked out of the room when she walked in. All chatting and joking stopped. She slid into the same seat as the day before.

Mr. Lenox entered and greeted everyone. Then he looked toward Jackson. "Oh, Mr. Wentworth?" Mr. Lenox looked down at his roll sheet, then back at Jackson again. "Jackson Wentworth?"

One of the boys in the back row lobbed a paper ball at Jackson.

"Yep," Jackson said without looking up from his screen.

"You missed the first day of class, Mr. Wentworth. Care to tell us why?"

"Nope."

The boys snickered, and even Cam felt a small smile on her face.

"Mr. Wentworth, you'll need to see me after class," Mr. Lenox said.

"Mr. Wentworth is my father," Jackson replied, clicking rapidly. "Maybe he'll need to join us."

Something flickered across Jackson's face, and then he shrugged.

Giving up, Mr. Lenox handed out a packet of information. "Part of this course is a project that you'll work on throughout the semester. You may pick your own partners."

Ugh, Cam thought. There was no one here she wanted to spend time with, let alone collaborate with on a semester-long project. She could only assume her classmates felt the same.

"By next week you need to let me know who you're working with. I'll need project outlines in four weeks," Mr. Lenox continued.

The project was open-ended—exactly the type of assignment she'd been hoping to get in this class. The objective was to create something that solved a problem. Each team would need to research the source of a problem and then create, test, and iterate a solution by the end of the term. It would count as half of their overall grade.

Mr. Lenox gave them the last five minutes of class to pair up and think about their projects. After reading through the instructions, Cam turned in her seat to see what the rest of the room was up to. She knew she was in trouble. The back-row boys were all in pairs, a few already talking about ideas. Jackson still clicked furiously on his laptop, seemingly unaware of what was happening.

Guess I found my partner, she thought.

Cam filled Vivian in after school in the stats classroom, where DECA met. Vivian was in charge of social media marketing for the team's cookie sales that year—a prized role and a big deal for a sophomore. "It's part of my three-year plan to be on the state exec board," Viv explained last summer. "Youngest social media manager in the whole state will look *super great* on my application. It's giving driven, it's giving organized, it's giving goal oriented." Then she'd done a chef's kiss in the air.

Cam often found herself hanging around while Viv made reels and memes about cookies, club activities, and other business things for DECA.

"Jackson Wentworth?" Viv said as she fluffed a cookie wrapper to get it just right. "I remember that guy. Doesn't really say much."

"Well, at least he didn't actively try to make me uncomfortable during class," Cam said.

"You've got a high bar there, Cam."

"I gotta start somewhere."

Viv adjusted the ring light she'd pointed toward the cookies and took some practice shots with her phone. "Okay, so Jackson Wentworth. I think he was in my fifth-grade class. Yeah, wait, he totally was! He was super into those cards, like Pokémon but not as cool. What were those?"

"Ooh." Cam had a sudden memory of the middle school cafeteria. A group of boys sat together to play cards with words and little drawings on them. Those kids didn't have a lot of social capital, but people pretty much left them alone. "Magic cards!"

"Right. That's it!" Vivian held her phone to her mouth. "Hey, Siri, what's the magic card game?"

Siri responded, "Magic: The Gathering is a trading-card game. Players buy and trade cards and build their own card decks."

"Thank you, queen." Vivian had a friendly only policy toward AI. *So they know I'm a friendly when they take over*, she always said. She scrolled through her phone to see what Siri pulled up. "Wow, this is really a whole thing."

"Let me see," Cam said as she leaned over so they could look together. "I mean, I collected Sillybandz when I was little. Is this like that?"

"No. I think this is, like, next level," Vivian replied. "Look, they meet in person and do battles and stuff."

"Well, whatever. I'm sure he doesn't do it anymore."

Vivian had a twinkle in her eye. "Oh my god. What if he does, and he won't be your partner unless you go do battle with him at a game store or whatever."

Cam shoved Viv's shoulder playfully. "Yeah, I'm sure that's what he's gonna do."

One of the DECA guys, a junior, opened the door. "When are you gonna be done in here, Knix? I gotta set up my staff training."

"Don't come for me unless I send for you, Damian. What did I say?" Viv snapped.

Damian disappeared, and the door clicked shut.

"Staff training?" Cam asked.

Viv rolled her eyes. "He's doing a hospitality simulation, and he's weak on employee engagement and retention."

Cam raised an eyebrow. "Right."

Viv waved a hand. "He's a cheap manager trying to cut corners. He doesn't understand the basic principle that investing in your staff will drive long-term revenue and minimize losses from turnover of new staff."

"I'm going to pretend I know what that means," Cam replied.

"Good plan," Viv said with a laugh. She paused, her brow furrowed. "Didn't Jackson's dad die or something? I feel like I remember something happening to his family."

Cam nodded. "His mom. I remember hearing about it in math in seventh grade. She had a heart attack on a plane, and they couldn't land in time. Died in the air."

Cam remembered kids whispering about it, which led to months of anxiety. It made her nervous that something might happen to her parents too. It was the first time she'd ever thought about what that would mean. To this day she still got nervous when one of them flew for work.

"Geez, that's so terrible," Viv said, taking some more shots with her phone. "I don't see him around much. Who does he hang with?"

"I'm not sure," Cam said, gathering up her things, "but I'll find out."

< br >

The next day Cam went on a hunt for Jackson. Each afternoon the school had office hours—open time when students could meet with teachers, work on group projects, or generally get things done. Where did gamer kids hang out? She asked a few people in passing if they'd seen him and got a tip: attic.

The building's attic level was a place Cam never went. Going upstairs as far as she could, she found herself in the art studio. It ran the length of the main building. The ceiling slanted like her attic at home, with huge skylight windows on both sides. It was deserted, and there definitely were not gamer kids hanging out. She turned to leave, but a small door caught her eye. There was a sign—LOUNGE, DEDICATED 1946.

She turned the knob cautiously and exposed an enclave of nerdom. There were beanbags strewn around the room and a few old tables set up with chairs on either side. Several boys were totally engrossed in their laptops. One was hooked into a VR headset in a corner. The space had a small, circular window on one end, like attics often do, and a single lightbulb hanging from the ceiling with a pull cord. Just as Cam began wondering why these guys were allowed here without an adult, Mr. Fitzgerald—a nearly retired, mostly aloof chemistry teacher—ambled past. He stopped and looked up from his papers, scanned the room, and then went on his way.

Looking around, Cam spotted Jackson sitting in a beanbag to her right. He was wearing big over-ear headphones and had a little lap desk propped under his computer.

"Um, hey, Jackson?"

His eyes darted to her briefly, and he did a double take. "What are you doin' here?"

"Hey, yeah, people told me you might be in here. I didn't even know this place existed!" Cam tried to sound conspiratorial in a *Hey, isn't this crazy?* way.

"Okay. I'm kinda busy." Jackson's attention was still focused on his laptop. He had a wireless mouse she hadn't noticed, and he clicked and typed furiously.

"Can you, like, pause it?" Cam asked.

He snorted. "You can't *pause* online play. It's live. You know, *online*."

She heard some snorts from around the room.

"Okay. I can wait for you to die or something," she offered. She dropped onto a stool nearby and started scrolling on her phone.

Jackson continued playing, but his eyes kept darting to her. With a sigh, he clicked a few more times and shut the laptop. "What do you want?"

"Hey! Yeah, so, Mr. Lenox was saying how we need to pick partners for the semester project?"

"Is that a question?"

"Well, no. He said that."

"Why did you ask it like a question?"

"Oh, um, I guess I didn't mean it like a question. I just . . . said it like a question."

Jackson just looked at her, expressionless.

"Anyway," she continued, "we need partners. And the rest of the class—I think they already paired up."

"So?"

"So I think we should be partners."

"Do I have a choice?"

"Not really." She shrugged. "But neither do I."

He shrugged back. "Okay. Fine. I don't like group work, though." He reopened his laptop and started clicking again.

She giggled nervously. "Cool. I mean, yeah, me neither. So I'll see you in class?"

"Probably."

"Okay, bye!" Cam waved and laughed nervously again. She got up and left the room.

< br >

That afternoon the whole school had an assembly to learn about spring club options. When Cam saw two juniors from her Intro to CS class take the stage, she sat up straighter and nudged Viv. "Those guys are in my CS class."

Viv looked judgmental. "I don't like them."

"Hey, everybody," the taller boy said. "I'm Jeremy."

The other boy leaned into the mic a little too far, so his voice boomed over the auditorium. "I'm Matt."

Everybody cringed.

"We're the copresidents of the RoboSub team."

Cam and Viv exchanged glances.

RoboSub? Viv mouthed.

"RoboSub is a competition where schools, mostly colleges actually, make an autonomous underwater vehicle, or AUV," Matt said.

"RoboSub gives us a theme and tasks every year, and then it's our job to build and program a submarine to do all the tasks," Jeremy explained.

"And fit the theme!" Matt added.

"So, yeah, we need some more guys to help us build the sub."

Cam's face crinkled up like she'd gotten a whiff of something rotten. *More guys?* She turned to Viv, who made the same face.

"We'll also need people who are good at getting sponsors and stuff," Jeremy said, "because the sub parts are expensive."

They looked at each other, out of things to say. After an awkward pause, Matt took the mic again and boomed, "Join RoboSub!"

Viv leaned toward Cam. "We are totally doing that."

"What?" Cam was interested in the concept but definitely did not want to spend more time with the guys from her class.

"This is exactly the type of thing that could help you learn more about code and stuff."

Before Cam could respond, a teacher waved at them from the end of the row and motioned for them to stop talking.

As soon as the presentations were over, Viv jumped up and grabbed Cam's hand. "Come on, let's go get info from their table."

Out in the hallway, the girls got to the RoboSub table before the copresidents had even made it there. There was a poster with pictures from the competition last year, but what really got Cam's attention was the largest object on the table: the autonomous underwater vehicle.

This was a serious robot. It didn't look like what sprang to mind when she thought *submarine*. All the wiring and electrical hardware was enclosed inside a large clear tube in the center of the robot. That made sense, because it needed to be submerged underwater, so it had to be leakproof. Cam knew it wasn't possible to control a cylindrical tube underwater, and surrounding it was hardware that made the whole structure look more like a generator. Propellers stuck out on both sides. Peering closely, Cam saw sloppy work: joints that needed better soldering, empty space that could be eliminated for speed and handling.

That manipulator could get a wider degree of reach if they adjusted the angle where it's attached, Cam thought.

There would be a lot of code involved, but looking at the machine, Cam felt at home. This included fabrication. She could do this.

"Oh, look at this," Viv said, picking up a pamphlet. "The competition is in San Diego. Cali, here we come!"

Cam cringed. "That sounds like an expensive trip. We've never even been to California for, like, a family trip."

"This says the funds for the sub and the trip all come from corporate sponsorships."

Cam's parents would be skeptical about a trip so far away. But they said they wanted to support her learning more about engineering. Maybe they'd consider it.

"You really think we should do this?" Cam asked, picking up another leaflet with a picture of a girl assembling some kind of electrical rig.

"Absolutely! Look. In addition to engineers, they need people to handle marketing and sponsorship. Each team has to make a movie about their sub that follows that year's theme. I can totally do that! Getting sponsors is just, like, networking, right? My dad always says that's important for people who want to work in business." Vivian had long dreamed of running her own company. "And next year when I do the entrepreneurship simulation for DECA, I'll have to know about fundraising."

"Hey, what's up?" Matt said, ambling up to the table. "Are you interested in RoboSub?"

"Yes, my friend and I are both interested," Viv said, grabbing Cam's arm.

"Oh, hey," Matt said, noticing Cam. "Aren't you in my CS class?"

"Yeah, it's my first year."

"I know," he said. His smile was friendly and open. "It's my second, and it's a small group. It can be a tough crowd, and Lenox can be kind of a drag. But there's a lot to learn."

Cam nodded. "I was kinda surprised, to be honest. I thought it was an intro class."

"I guess it is," he said. "But I think you're the only sophomore this year. Oh, and that kid Jackson if he doesn't drop."

"You think he will?" she asked.

He shrugged. "I'm not sure he'll be able to keep up. You have to teach yourself a lot in that class. Lenox is there more to answer questions."

She had definitely picked up on that vibe.

"So, what can I tell you about RoboSub?" Matt asked.

She had so many questions, she wasn't sure where to start.

Luckily Viv had no such doubt. "So the fundraising and sponsorships—how are they judged at the competition?"

"Ah, yeah. We're not great at that part, to be honest. There are basically two ways we're judged: how the AUV performs and how we present ourselves as a team. We get scored on our strategy video, design report, and a presentation about all that stuff. We always end up kinda crunched for time with the AUV, so we don't spend much time on the rest. And sponsorships are super important—all the parts for the sub are pricey, and the travel to the competition is too."

Cam flipped through one of the pamphlets that detailed the scoring rubric. There were lots of performance tasks evaluated live in San Diego.

"What happens if something breaks during one of the runs?" she asked.

Matt grinned. "That's the most fun. There's a really great community at the TRANSDEC—people help each other out.

You're given some time to try and fix what went wrong between runs."

Jeremy arrived at the table and looked surprised to see Cam and Viv. "Sorry. We can't give those pamphlets away—we only have a few," he said, taking a swig from a giant Arizona iced tea.

"Oh, sorry." Cam started to put it back, but Viv stopped her.

"We're going to join the club, so we need these for our parents. It says here that all members need to be in San Diego for the competition this summer. We need to check that with our parents before we can sign up." Her tone made it clear she wasn't asking.

"Well, the trip's not a given. We might have limited spots if lots of people sign up. A free trip to San Diego is a pretty big draw," Jeremy said.

Cam looked around. Other clubs, like School Spirit League and Key Club, had large crowds of students around their tables. Only Cam and Viv were at this one. And besides, Viv intervening gave Cam's brain time to kick in.

I'm interested in this stuff, she thought. *I'm not just some rando looking for a free trip.*

"We'll take our chances," Viv countered, giving him a steely glare. "If you end up making some sort of selection, I would love to know what the parameters are to narrow down the candidates." Viv's mom was a surgeon, and her father was a big deal at some company Cam didn't really understand. It led to Viv sometimes throwing around fancy language. It always amused Cam when Viv used it to rattle teachers. Hearing her use it now made Cam want to give her friend a hug.

Matt had opened his mouth to respond, and judging from the look on his face, he was going to be friendly. But Jeremy spoke first. "We kinda need people who have experience with this sort of thing. Six months isn't much time to finish the project," he said.

"Perfect. Cam is in your CS class," Viv said, giving Cam's arm a little tug. "And she's a maker. Right, Cam?"

Cam's cheeks felt hot. "I fabricate, yeah. I'm pretty familiar with electronics and some robotics. Perception, manipulation, locomotion—"

"That's awesome!" Matt said. "I think we could pick up some points there this year. Our hardware team could use some help."

Jeremy shot a look at Matt, which shut him up. "The competition is in late July, so you have to be able to work on the sub after school is out."

"That works for us. We have no plans," Viv said.

Cam struggled to find words. What she had already said was true: she knew a lot about hardware and felt confident she could make the sub better, even after just looking at it on the surface. But Jeremy was so dismissive. So confident that she couldn't possibly know anything. It made Cam doubt herself. What was that term she read about the other day? *Imposter syndrome.*

Jeremy played with the tab on his tea can and made it clear he was bored by the conversation. "Whatever. We'll have to see if there's space."

Viv crossed her arms—not a look Cam ever wanted to be on the receiving end of. "The odds seem good. Your friend here says you need help from someone like Cam. And I'm joining the team for marketing and sponsorship, which you mentioned specifically as a highlighted need in your presentation."

Jeremy just looked at her. Viv looked right back.

Matt's head pinged between the two of them, then he pulled out a paper with numbered lines on it. "Here, leave your names and emails, and we'll be in touch with info about the first meeting."

Jeremy shot him a look, and Matt cleared his throat. "Uh, if there is a meeting. I mean, if we have enough people. Er, not enough people."

Viv leaned over to write her name. "Thanks," she said. "We look forward to it."

Cam quickly scribbled her name and email and shuffled away. They went into a small hallway to debrief.

"Oh my god. That was intense," Cam said.

Viv shrugged. "I eat dudes like that for breakfast."

"When have you ever encountered a dude like that?" Cam countered, using air quotes.

"Just now, and I destroyed him with my wit."

"Do you really want to be on the team?" Cam asked, flipping through the pamphlet she still clutched in her hands. "It looks like a ton of work."

"Of course I do!" Viv replied. "Look, a free trip to San Diego is no joke. Maybe we can look at colleges while we're out there. According to the statistics you quoted yesterday, I'm willing to bet there aren't many girls in clubs like this. It's almost college application time, sister!"

Cam laughed. "I know. I just don't want you to spend so much time if it's only for me."

Vivian turned serious. "First of all, doing something with you would be a great way to spend my time. I'm here for you. And second, like I said—this'll look great on my DECA exec application. And I'll be able to get a head start with experience for next year's ICDC."

Cam knew that was the big year-end DECA conference. She had even memorized what it stood for: International Career Development Conference. She did things for Viv too. Cam smiled, grateful for her friend. "Okay. Yeah. Let's do it."

Having Vivian with her definitely increased Cam's confidence about joining the club, but she couldn't deny the sinking feeling in her stomach. It was clear that Jeremy didn't want them there.

Being on the team would give Cam the chance to design

and create on a whole new level. She could never afford that tech on her own, and she'd never been able to build on this scale before. Looking at the sub made her head spin with ideas—there was so much to do, and she was eager. The best way to figure out if she should study engineering or robotics in college was to try it now.

So was she willing to put up with Jeremy for the rest of the year and even part of her summer?

Yeah. She totally was.

```
(function imposter(){
    console.log("Chapter");
    console.log("Four");
})();
```

Chapter Four

Cam sat down next to Jackson the next day in class. He was, as always, playing a game.

"Hey," she said.

"Hey," he said without looking up.

"Can we talk about our project?"

"Sure."

"I think it'd be easier if you got off that for a second."

Hearing her tone, he sighed and quit. He closed the laptop and turned to face her. "Sorry."

"So, our project," she said. "Our outline will be due sooner than we think."

"Yeah. I wanna make a game."

"A game?"

"Yeah, an MMO."

"MM what?"

"A massively multiplayer online game."

She gave him a blank look.

"You know, like *CoD* or *Fortnite*."

"Well, the only parameter of the project is to research and solve a problem," she said.

"So?"

"So how would a new version of *Fortnite* solve a problem?"

He shrugged and crossed his arms. "I don't know. But I took this class to learn to make my own games."

"You can still do that, but maybe not for this project."

"Well, what's your idea?"

"I don't really have one. I just want to make sure we follow the guidelines. Maybe we should start with a problem first?"

"Fine."

"Okay. Are there any problems in the world that you think about?"

"Nope."

Cam didn't think Mr. Lenox would accept an online shooter game. And the only issue she'd thought about lately was, well . . .

"I have something," she said.

"What?"

"Well, I've been doing some research about women in tech and engineering."

Jackson fiddled with his pen. "Okay."

"It's actually a huge problem. Women face really intense discrimination, hazing, passive aggression—all kinds of stuff. It makes some people quit, which means fewer women in the fields. And girls don't see role models and don't want to be the only one. It creates this cycle where fewer women pursue STEM, and those who do can't get hired or they quit because it sucks."

"Whoa. That was a lot," Jackson replied.

"I know. Isn't it ridiculous?"

He sighed. "Well, what could we possibly do about that? We're just two high schoolers."

"I guess I don't know yet," Cam replied. "Do you have a different idea?"

"No."

"So what do we do?"

Cam wasn't sure her idea was practical for the assignment, but she knew the issue mattered and was a real issue in the world. Mr. Lenox hadn't asked them to think big picture, but he hadn't provided many guidelines at all. If Jackson didn't have any ideas, they were left with Cam's.

"Let's think on it and meet tomorrow during office hours. I can come to the attic again."

He sat up straighter. "No, don't do that."

"Why not?" Cam asked.

"Some of the guys—after you left—wondered why you came up there."

"I came to talk to you."

"I know that. But they're guys, so it was just... I don't know. I don't think we should meet there."

She could tell he was leaving something out but decided not to push. Class was over in two minutes. "Okay, fine. Let's meet at Aldo's on Thursday."

"Okay."

The bell rang, and they gathered their bags.

< br >

Viv had cookie-sale duty that afternoon, so Cam perched on the wall behind her and did homework.

"Don't come sniffing around here without cash, Nathan. I know your tricks!" Viv quipped at a freshman who lurked a few feet from the table. He mumbled something about leftovers and scurried away.

"Did you pick a project for CS?" Viv asked Cam.

"We talked about women in STEM, actually," Cam told her.

"Yesss! I love that for you! Jackson is okay with it?"

"I think so," Cam replied.

"That's pretty cool of him."

"Yeah?"

"Yeah. I mean, what does he know or care about women in professional industries? He spends more time interacting with dudes online than he does with real people. Especially female people."

"True. He also told me not to come to the attic again. He got all weird about it."

"Maybe the attic guys think you two are dating and gave him a hard time."

"Who knows. He's, like, impossible to read. I never know what he's thinking. I'm like, *Do you hate me? Are we chill?* He's willing to talk to me and stuff for class, so I guess that's nice."

"Nice or indifferent?" Viv countered.

"Either way, I'll take it." Cam laughed. "The more I read about the women in engineering stuff, the more I think even indifference is nicer than what most women deal with."

"It's definitely nicer than what you're dealing with. Speaking of, did that Jeremy guy say anything to you in class?"

"Nope. He totally ignored me."

"Great," Viv said. "I consider that an improvement."

"Hey, ladies. What are we servin' up today?" Liz, a junior, approached the table.

"Double chocolate chip, my friend. A little birdie told me that's your fave," Viv said, bagging a cookie. Handing it across the table, Viv leaned in and lowered her voice. Cam could barely make it out when Viv said, "Did you get the info?"

"Only one other name on the list," Liz reported, taking her cookie. Cam noticed she didn't pay for it.

"Excellent. You always got my back, girlie," Viv said.

Liz took a bite of the cookie. "Anything for my cookie hookup. You know I got you."

"What was that about?" Cam asked when Liz walked away.

"She works in the Student Activities Office. I had her check the sign-up list for the RoboSub thing. Sounds like we're in!"

"Wait. You gave her a bribe cookie?"

"Whoa, whoa, whoa," Viv said, looking around. "First of all, don't go throwing out phrases like 'bribe cookie' in public. This is an entrepreneurial enterprise for DECA and is very, very aboveboard. My books are balanced, girl." She leaned in. "Second, you know I've got my little birds all over this school. Mama's gotta keep those seeds flowin' so eyes and ears stay open. You know what I mean?"

Cam laughed. "I think you've been watching too much *Game of Thrones*."

"I think *you're* watching too little." Viv checked the time and started cleaning up. "Anyway, if there was only one other sign-up, they have to let us in. They need the help, and there's no excuse. San Diego, here we come!"

Cam was excited—a trip to San Diego with Viv sounded great, and the team met in the design lab. Still, Jeremy's hostility bothered her.

"What if he doesn't tell us about the first club meeting?" Cam asked.

"I'd like to see him try," Viv said, knowing instantly who Cam was talking about. "I'd like him to give me one reason to march straight into the principal's office and file a complaint." She snapped the cookie money box shut. "One. Little. Reason."

< br >

Later that week, Cam went to Aldo's and set up her laptop. She hadn't come up with any new earth-shattering ideas. The pressure was on to decide fast. They couldn't start outlining until they knew what they would do.

Jackson slumped into the chair across from her and looked around. "Hey," he said.

"Hey!" Cam replied. "How are you?"

Jackson nodded. "Yeah, fine, good."

"Do you wanna order food or anything?" she asked.

"Nah, I'm good," he said. "I've been thinking about the project."

"Oh, awesome!" Cam was glad she wouldn't have to do all the brainstorming.

"I like RPGs."

"RBG? I didn't know there were games about her. I guess that could be connected to the women-in-STEM thing."

Jackson looked confused. "What? No. RPG. Role-playing games."

She wasn't sure where he was going. "So you want to make one of those?"

"I mean, that's what I *wanted* to do before we had to partner up. I wanna code games."

She ignored the disdain in his voice. "Well, what would that even look like? A young professional woman interacting with people at work? What would she fight?"

He shrugged. Cam waited. Finally Jackson mumbled something.

"What?" she asked.

"I don't know. She could fight, like, jerks. We'd come up with a name for them." He paused. "I made a call."

"A call?" *I'm not following this at all*, she thought.

Jackson looked at her for a moment, then pulled some papers out of his bag and put them on the table. "I was thinking about what you said in class yesterday, so I called my sister. She works out in LA, for some dating app start-up thing."

"You have a sister?" Cam had grown up with Jackson but didn't remember anything about a sister.

He nodded. "She's a lot older. Anyway, I told her about how you wanted to do our project on women in technology or whatever—"

"Women in STEM fields, yeah."

"Whatever. And she, like, erupted into all this stuff about the guys she works with, and how messed up their behavior is. How she and her friends have to tolerate it, but it's this total double standard because the guys get to do whatever they want, and Willa and her friends feel like they do all the work. And she said . . ." He stopped and leaned back in his chair. Fiddled with the papers.

"She said?" Cam prodded.

"She said one of the guys brushed her ass once when they were leaving a meeting."

"Oh my god! What did she do?"

Jackson looked embarrassed but also angry. "She reported it to her boss, but nothing happened."

"That's gross!"

He nodded and sat up straighter. "Yeah, it's fucked up." He cleared his throat. "So anyway, I don't know what we can do about it, but I like games. And I, you know . . . I know how they work. So I drew some character sketches."

The first sketch was a woman—based on Jackson's sister, if Cam had to guess. She wore professional clothing, tied-back hair, practical shoes, and carried a laptop. The second sketch was of the same woman but transformed—her laptop was a shield, her hair fell freely in waves around her shoulders, and her shoes were awesome knee-high boots just like Wonder Woman's. Unlike Wonder Woman, though, this character actually had pants—practical black leggings that disappeared into the boots—a belt, and a top, sort of like a button-down shirt but cooler. She looked ready to kick some major corporate ass.

Cam laughed. "This is awesome!"

Jackson blushed. "Thanks. And I did this one too. This is maybe what we could use as like, you know, the Goombas."

"Goombas?"

"The bad mushrooms from Super Mario? Like a generic bad guy all over the place that's relatively easy to defeat. We would need to come up with a name for them."

The image was a man in business attire with an overly large mouth and enormous hands.

"I get the hands, but what's with the mouth?"

"My sister said the worst thing about these guys is that they talk over women and steal their ideas."

"Not the ass brushing?"

He leaned in. "I was thinking the ass brushing could be a health hit, and the interrupting could actually freeze the player and create XP and time loss, making the level even harder."

"XP?" Cam asked.

"Experience points."

"Clever," Cam said and laughed again. "And the time loss?"

Jackson's blush deepened. "My sister said she feels added pressure to advance quickly, because she wants to have kids. I guess there's all this research that says women fall behind in their careers when they do that or whatever."

Cam took some notes. "I could look into that."

Jackson nodded. "And you know, the point of the game will be to get control of the company—to defeat the big boss, an uber-version of these guys. Defeat him, and you get to run your own company. Each level could be timed. When these guys talk over the player, she'll lose time, and it'll make the level harder. There could be an overall time bank for the whole game, because of the motherhood thing."

"That should probably be optional."

"Sure. We can set that up. It can be a harder mode maybe—or an extra objective."

Cam had to admit the concept was cool, and they could use her research. She'd need to talk to more women and read more online. It was something they could code, and Jackson actually seemed interested in it. She loved that the main character was female. She'd often thought she would probably like gaming more if she could play as a girl—it seemed like the options were usually male or some kind of alien creature thing.

"Jackson, this is . . ." She paused, searching for the right word.

He watched her face and began to gather the papers. "You think it's stupid. That's fine. It's just an idea. I don't even know about this stuff. I was just talking to my sister because it was her birthday or whatever. But we can just—"

"Wait!" She put a hand on the image of the superhero business lady. "I don't think it's a stupid idea. I think it's really cool, actually."

Jackson froze. "You do?"

"Yeah. It's funny, and it draws attention to your sister's issues. I mean, the details need ironing out—"

"We could do that in the level storyboarding."

"—and it's obviously an oversimplification of the problem, but I think it's a place to start. My one question is, how does it address the assignment objective?"

"What do you mean?"

"Mr. Lenox says we have to address a societal problem *and* try to fix it. This definitely spreads awareness, but how does it fix the problem?"

"Well, I was thinking we could donate any profits."

"To whom?"

"I don't know. There must be organizations that fight against this stuff. I had two different girls tell me about it in one day, so it can't be that under the radar."

The more Cam thought about it, the more she liked his suggestion. "I could do some research about organizations that work on behalf of women in STEM industries." Remembering the way she'd doubted herself in class and at the club fair, she had another idea. "We should create a penalty for imposter syndrome too."

"Imposter what?" Jackson asked.

"Imposter syndrome. It's a feeling that underrepresented people get—especially in STEM fields. A feeling that we shouldn't be there—in class, at a job, in a club—even though we're qualified. You know, feeling like imposters in those places. And it's messed up, because, like, it comes from society in general and also from some people making others feel unwelcome. Like your sister's coworkers." *Or our classmates*, she wanted to add.

"Right, yeah," Jackson said. "That makes sense. I mean, it's fucked up. But I get it." He gathered his drawings and put them back in his bag. "We can talk mechanics and storyline next week. I'm going to work on the artwork, because we can attach the sprites to whatever we code."

"Sprites?"

"You know . . . the character images. You attach them to the coded objects."

"Ooooh. Mm-hmm, sprites. Got it." Cam laughed nervously. "I thought you said *mites*, so I was like, huh?" She was totally bluffing, and he could totally tell.

Jackson smiled. "Right." He started to walk away, then turned back. "Hey, have you heard of the Processing Foundation?"

She shook her head. "Nope."

"You should check it out this weekend. They have lots of free content about coding. If you happen to know someone who needs a place to get started." He looked at her.

"Thanks."

The Processing Foundation. Processing Foundation. Processing Foundation.

As soon as he was out of sight, she pulled up her Notes app and typed in the name. She knew what she'd do this weekend.

```
(function imposter(){
    console.log("Chapter");
    console.log("Five");
})();
```

Chapter Five

Cam had a few hours before Vivian showed up for their sleepover. Scrolling through the Processing Foundation website, she was immediately comforted by the part of their mission that said: "Our goal is to support people of all backgrounds in learning how to program and make creative work with code, especially those who might not otherwise have access to tools and resources."

Perfect, she thought.

On her way downstairs to grab the printer, she overheard her parents in the kitchen.

"I'm worried about her," her mom said. "First the class, and now this robot club. Remember what happened to my cousin Alexendra?"

Cam stopped in her tracks. *Who is Alexendra?*

Her dad sighed. "That was a very different situation. The class is where Cam wants to be. If we try to stop her, she'll only want it more. That's what all those parenting books say anyway."

Cam stifled a laugh. *Parenting books?*

"Maybe there's another way for her to explore this," Mom said. "It's not worth the trouble with these boys, and the teacher doing nothing. What if this is just a passing interest? We could find a camp or a summer program..."

Cam slipped past the kitchen, took the printer, and returned to her room. Her mind raced.

I don't want to do a summer program. I want to study CS at school. And why shouldn't I? Who is Alexendra, and what does she have to do with any of this?

Cam's phone buzzed. A text from Viv. **Be there in an hour.**

Shrugging off the distractions, she connected the printer and got to work.

Cam was still deep in her notes about p5, JavaScript, and Python when Vivian showed up.

"Whoa," Viv said. "Are you trying to solve a murder in here?"

Cam had been lost in her work. Papers surrounded her, many covered with scribbles. The entire reference of commands for p5 was on her right. *I'll memorize them, like vocab in French class*, she'd thought. That led to scattered index cards behind her. Reading the commands presented another roadblock: she didn't know what they meant. *Okay, URL. I know what that is. Frame rate? Bezier?* So then she'd started googling and making note cards for *those* words, and looking around now she realized it had all gotten sort of out of hand.

"I found some resources to get started with coding," she gushed, finishing the last of her structure cards. "Well, Jackson told me about them. It's like learning whole languages!"

Vivian joined her on the floor. "I mean, that makes sense. It's basically a language to talk to a computer, right?"

"Right. And there are different languages depending on what you want to say."

Viv looked confused.

"It's like . . ." Cam looked around and grabbed a paper with a 3D coordinate plane on it. "What is this?"

"A box?" Viv answered like it was a trick question.

"Right. It's a box. So p5 is a visual language. It's good for shapes and colors, drawing objects, making them move. Stuff like that."

"Okay . . ."

"But I wouldn't use p5 if I want to build an app for my phone. See what I mean?"

"Not really."

"It's like if you could only order food in French but not Spanish."

"What could I do in Spanish?"

"I don't know—gardening."

"Uh-huh . . ."

"You can make visuals in p5, so I would use it for any situation where I want to do that. But if I want to make an app, I might use Python or Java."

"So there are lots of languages. Learning one won't be enough?"

"Definitely not. But I guess it depends on what I want to do."

"Geez," Viv said, glancing around again.

"I need to pick a language to start with, so I picked p5. Once I understand more about the mechanics, I'll need to go beyond that."

"Well," Viv said, gathering up some note cards and making a pile. "I guess we better get to work."

A few hours later Vivian took a break while Cam watched tutorials online.

"Do you think Dylan is back on the market yet?" Viv asked.

Cam looked up at Viv scrolling through Dylan's TikTok. She shrugged. "I don't know. He's been dating Maria since, like, middle school."

Viv sighed. "I feel like all the guys worth dating were snapped up in, like, eighth grade, and now their girlfriends have vise grips on them forever. We totally missed the window."

Cam snorted. "I think I was too busy playing games on *Roblox* to notice the window opened in the first place." Cam had spent many hours as her avatar in virtual worlds, but she never designed her own games in Creator Hub. Vivian wasn't into it, and when Cam dipped her toe into other games as she got older, people made weird comments in the chat when they realized she was a girl. It gave her the ick, so she turned to making and fabrication instead. Now that she was learning about how women were excluded—mostly through social pressure—from computer science and engineering, she wished she could tell younger Cam to mute the chat and do whatever she wanted.

"That's what I mean!" Viv sat up. "Cam, you cannot turn sixteen without ever kissing someone. There are literally movies made about this. That's how big of a tragedy it is."

"Hey, leave me alone! We can't all go to sleepaway camp and practice with people we'll never see again."

Viv put her phone down. "Yes, yes. I agree I had an unfair advantage."

"Living in a small town doesn't help either."

Viv nodded. "But still. It's not like there are *no* options."

Cam didn't like her tone. "What are you getting at?"

"Well, you do have this new *partner* situation."

"Viv, no! I'm not interested."

"I mean, he could be cute, with a little Fab Five makeover. It's not like there's a ton that needs to be done. Little personal grooming. Little transition to clothes that actually fit."

"No. Thanks."

Viv shrugged. "Okay, fine! But I haven't given up on you." She resumed scrolling. "Do you think Dylan prefers girls who wear beanies?"

The girls studied until one in the morning and finally fell asleep on top of Cam's covers. When her dad opened the door, Cam felt like she'd been asleep for ten minutes.

"Good morning, girls!" he said, entering. "Whoa. What happened in here?" He put his hands on his hips. "Are you trying to solve cold cases? I knew I shouldn't have let you listen to *Serial*."

Cam groaned and rolled over, waving a hand at her dad. "Too early. Must sleep more."

Vivian grunted in approval.

"It's almost eleven! I made pancakes and hot coffee." He came over to the bed to wave his cup around near their faces.

Vivian sat up like Frankenstein's monster with her eyes closed. "Must. Consume. Coffee."

"Come on down. Pot's hot and ready!"

Rolling off the bed, the girls picked their way through the papers still littered across the floor.

"Here they come!" Mom said, pouring two cups of coffee and giving Cam a kiss on the head. "You caught me just in time. I've got two open houses today." She handed the cups to the girls. "I could always use some help if you two wanted to make some extra cash. There's lots that needs doing to get houses ready to show."

Cam refrained from rolling her eyes. When she was younger, her mom often brought her to open houses to help with all the last-minute sprucing up before a showing—placing plants, chopping pillows just right, opening windows, and sticking the sign at the end of the driveway.

"These two really burned the midnight oil last night," her dad said, saving them from having to politely turn down her mom.

"Oh, really? What were you up to?" her mom asked.

"Oh, you know," Viv said, adding cream to her coffee. "Doomscrolling. Talking about boys. The usual."

"It doesn't look like the usual," Dad countered. "I haven't seen a bedroom floor like that since I wrote my senior thesis."

Cam sipped her black coffee. "I was studying."

"Studying?" Mom asked as she served Cam two piping-hot pancakes. "On a Friday night? I swear, you kids never get a break."

"I *thought* we would have a break, Mrs. G, but when I got here last night, our Cam was deep in a cram-sesh," Vivian said, pouring syrup over her steaming breakfast.

"Do you have a test coming up soon?" Dad asked.

"No. It's just that I realized a lot of other kids in my CS class already know some coding languages, so I need to catch up," Cam said. "We had to partner up for the semester-long project, and my partner told me about a website where I could start to learn more code."

Her dad looked at her mom and then turned to the girls. "This partner sounds nice," he said.

Vivian snorted.

"Is he not nice?" her mother asked, fixing Cam with an intense look.

"He's not *not* nice," Cam offered. "He doesn't seem to hate my guts like the other guys in class."

Her mom's jaw tightened.

"Well, to hate your guts he'd have to look up from *Fortnite* or whatever," Vivian said.

"What's this fellow's name?" Cam's father asked.

"Jackson."

Dad nodded. "Good name."

Now Cam did roll her eyes. Never had she brought home a romantic interest, and never would she. Her progressive parents had given her "the talk" when she was eleven, and it horrified her still. There was absolutely nothing between her and Jackson, but her parents were aggressively supportive—they couldn't wait for her to bring someone home so they could love and accept them. Her mom said she wanted Cam to have "a healthy sexual identity." Big cringe.

"Oh, he's not a candidate for our dear Cam's heart, Mr. G," Viv said.

"But he will be a good project partner, this Jackson?" Mom asked, packing some folders into her work bag.

"I hope so," Cam replied. "This project is worth half our grade. He actually came up with kind of a cool idea." She told them about the game Jackson proposed and what his sister said.

Cam's dad shook his head and exchanged a look with her mom, who looked down at her work bag. The pause was awkward. Cam's mother *always* had something to say.

What is up with her lately? Cam wondered.

Dad cleared his throat and turned back to the girls. "I wish I were surprised by what Jackson's sister said. I'm still sorry to hear it. Nobody deserves that kind of treatment. I'm glad you're planning to speak up about it." He glanced at Cam's mom again.

Cam could tell he was trying to be discreet, but her mom looked away and seemed nervous. *This is so weird*, Cam thought, *especially coming from Mom.*

"Yeah. He said his sister was really excited when she heard we might do it." Cam finished her last bite and stood up. "Let's get back to it, Viv."

"Will I see you after the open house is over?" her mom asked. Cam often went by to help her mom tidy and pack up.

"Yep. I'll see you there. Leave me the address?"

Mom came over to give her a kiss on the head. "Okay. See you later, nena."

Back in her room, Cam moved her cursor around and watched an oval obediently follow. She made a small adjustment to her code, and the oval turned orange.

Her dad knocked, then poked his head in. "Hey, girls. I don't mean to interrupt, but I was doing a little research of my own, and I found an organization you might be interested in. It's called Girls Who Code."

He came in and read from his iPad: "Girls Who Code is on a mission to close the gender gap in technology and to change the image of what a programmer looks like and does."

"Let me see that," Viv said, reaching for the iPad.

She brought it over to Cam and they scrolled the site together. It had lots of research, including a statistic that said in 1995, 37 percent of computer scientists were women, but that number had since dropped to 24 percent. Without action, that number would continue to drop. Most girls give up on computer science between the ages of thirteen and seventeen—high school, in other words—leaving only 4 percent involvement by girls in college computer science programs.

"They have summer programs for girls who want to get involved," Dad said. "And they do a lot of work in schools."

An image caught Cam's eye: five people, but they didn't look like any character she'd ever seen in a game. The tall, grotesquely curved women in games were one of the reasons Cam had lost interest in gaming as she got older. Why did female superheroes look like Barbie with a proton blaster? Where were the characters who looked like regular people?

It said "Girls Who Code Girls" on the image. There was a link that said "Code your own character now!" Cam clicked it.

Futuristic robotic music played, and a female voice said, "Seventy-seven percent of video game developers are men— meaning the majority of female and non-binary characters are designed by men. No wonder we're misrepresented."

Cam tapped through and was taken to a character-design page, like the one in *The Sims*. Except this had an open code space and prompts to make adjustments to characters. Cam read, "These tutorials will guide you through CSS, HTML, JavaScript and Python." Exactly what she was looking for.

The first window was for customizing the body:

```
01   Class Avatar:
02       body_type="......"
03       hip_type="......"
04       chest_type"......"
05
06   new_Avatar = Avatar( )
```

A blinking cursor signaled she could type in the missing values for body, hip, and chest type, or she could click on the blank space and see options: large, medium, and small. The avatar on screen morphed as she manipulated the code. A small label in the lower left corner told Cam which programming language she was using: Python.

Viv pulled up the workspace on her phone too. "Ohmigod, look. I can add my freckles!"

She'd found the next window, for changing the avatar's face:

```
01   /* CODE YOUR SKIN TONE, EYES,
     NOSE, LIPS & MORE */
02
03   .skin {
04       height: 160px;
05       width: 160px;
06       skin-color: .........;
07       skin-specificity: .........;
```

The /* symbol marked the beginning of a comment: a way to leave notes within the code that wouldn't be read by the browser. The skin color options ranged from dark to fair, and they could add details like acne and freckles. The hint at the bottom told Cam this was another coding language: CSS.

Cam laughed at Viv's excitement, delighted that her friend's freckles were an option, and that she was *interested* in coding her own avatar. It was easy to change the different features on a character—option menus opened in each place. And she noticed more than that: the code surrounding each option. Already she was becoming familiar with the syntax of coding languages. Each function on a clean new line, parentheses and quotation marks around customizable data, semicolons after each statement. *This is what character code looks like*, she thought.

Cam suddenly remembered her dad was still standing there. "Dad, this is amazing," she said. "Thank you so much."

"No problem," he said, heading back toward the door with his iPad back in his hand. "I saw there's a donate button too. I think you said you and Jackson want to donate your game profits somewhere, right?"

"Maybe this could be it, Cam!" Viv said, changing her character's hair color from green to purple. "I mean, if these people can get me off TikTok for even three minutes, they're onto something."

She had a point. "Really, Dad. This is so good. Thank you."

He smiled and backed out of the room, a proud glow on his face.

< br >

Around noon Vivian rolled off Cam's bed. "My mom says I need to come home for lunch. Gotta go."

"Thanks for helping me," Cam said, getting up to say goodbye.

"No problem." Viv hugged her friend. "And, hey, if it helps wipe the stupid smirk off that Jeremy guy's stupid face, then I'm here for it."

Cam laughed. *I wouldn't mind ending that smirk either*, she thought. But that wasn't why she was working so hard.

When she opened her laptop, a sea of letters, numbers, and symbols swam across the screen. In class so far, it had all been gibberish. It was starting to make sense, organizing into rows and sections. Already she could look at a few lines and *see* what it described.

```
function draw() {
  background(220);
  fill('purple');
  ellipse(150, 150, 280, 180)
}
```

She read the code block, and she *saw* a purple oval. She had a knack for this. And the more she read about how hard it was for girls, the more she wanted to show everyone, including herself, that she could do it. She *knew* she could.

It turned out that p5 wasn't complicated. It even used a lot of the same vocabulary as math. Setting up and manipulating shapes on a coordinate was something Cam had done since elementary school. Now she was doing it on a virtual plane on her computer.

The games Jackson played didn't appeal to Cam. Weird comments from other gamers aside, the characters didn't look like her. She didn't want to play as some random guy, and shooter games were uninteresting. She tried simulation and RPGs she could play by herself. Girls Who Code said 77 percent of engineers in the gaming industry were men. If life were *The Sims*, she'd make a character with geek and overachiever traits and do whatever she wanted.

But in real life Cam still dreaded going to computer science. Even though it was something she was passionate about.

Even though she thought it wouldn't be too hard once she got into it. Even though she had earned the right to take it like everybody else. In real life she didn't feel welcome. And everyone else was so confident—so sure she didn't belong. *Maybe they're right.* Maybe she really was an imposter.

An alarm buzzed—time to meet her mom at the open house.

< br >

Dad had to get the car's oil changed, so he dropped Cam off and said, "See you for dinner!"

Things were quiet at the house. *Hopefully that's because everyone already left,* Cam thought. She found her mom tucking a bunch of handouts into a folder.

"Ah, great! You're just in time. The last potential buyers just left," her mom said. She glowed.

Cam knew the drill by now: pack up the staging décor, tidy up anything people might have nudged or dropped, and pack up the car. Cam's mother's phone rang while they worked. Hands full of open house materials, she answered it and tapped the speaker button with her nose.

"Hey, Shane," she said. Shane was the new general manager at the real estate brokerage—Mom's new boss.

"Gabi! I need you to cover over on Goshen. Maurice is sick."

"Oh, I can't. Sorry about that. My husband has a—"

"Gabi, Gabi. I know it's short notice, but you're the only one available. Everyone else has showings all day. You know how Saturdays are."

Cam's mom put down the folders and leaned on the counter. "Well, that's just it, Shane, I'm not available. I was just saying that my husband—"

"Gabi, I hear you. But my hands are tied here. We have to cover the open house."

Why can't he cover it? Cam wondered. There was commotion in the background with people laughing. Then they heard Shane, muted as if he was leaning away or putting a hand over the phone, say, "I'll be right there. Don't let them play through. Two minutes."

Cam raised an eyebrow at her mom. *Play through?* she mouthed.

Golf, Mom mouthed back.

"So, Gabi, thank you so much for handling it."

"Shane. I have not agreed to—"

The call ended.

"Well, he seems nice," Cam said. Her mom had a great boss named Margaret for several years. But she moved to New York. Mom had tried to get the general manager job, but the brokerage had passed her over for Shane—a younger, whiter, male agent new to the firm.

Mom let out a frustrated "Ugh!" and put the phone on the counter. Closing her eyes, she took a deep breath and drummed her fingers on the counter. "Dad has softball today," she said.

Cam's dad was in a league with other middle-aged men from their town. It was very dorky and cute. Her mom went to every game and cheered, and when she was younger, Cam went too.

"I'm sure he'll understand," Cam said.

Mom's frustration was palpable. She slipped into the Spanish she used when she was most emotional. "¡Chuleta! No puedo ni trabajar por ese awebao."

Cam understood her mother but didn't respond. Instead she wondered aloud, "Could you just ignore him?" Cam knew that being a real estate agent meant her mother kind of worked for herself, but she was also affiliated with the larger real estate group.

Her mom shook her head. "He'll make it worse if I do. It's not worth the trouble. Jacquelina had issues with him a few weeks ago when she tried that." She pinched the bridge of her nose and closed her eyes. "This fool doesn't even do showings anymore. He just plays golf and skims his commission off the rest of us."

"That's so shitty," Cam said, feeling outraged. Her mom didn't deserve that.

"Gracias, nena," Mom replied. "I'll just have to do it and see if I can catch the end of the game."

They grabbed the rest of the boxes and headed out to the car.

When they got home and were almost done unloading the car, Mom turned to Cam. "Have I ever told you about my cousin Alexendra?"

"No," Cam said, trying to hide the excitement in her voice. "Who's she?"

Before Mom could respond, Cam's dad pulled into the driveway and honked. Mom waved at him. "A story for another time."

That night after dinner, a notification popped up on Cam's computer. New email from Jackson.

Thought you might want this. You said you want to do this club, right?

He had forwarded a message from Jeremy. The first Robo-Sub meeting was Monday.

Cam and Vivian were not on the email.

```
(function imposter(){
    console.log("Chapter");
    console.log("Six");
})();
```

Chapter Six

"I'm starting to really freakin' hate that guy," Viv said the next morning at her locker. "Did Jackson even sign up for the club?"

"No," Cam said. She'd asked Jackson the same question earlier. "I looked back at the list—they included everyone in our CS class."

"No. They didn't include *everyone* in CS." Viv fumed. "*You're* in that class. They included the *guys*. I'm going to punch that dude straight in the face."

Cam laughed. "No, you're not. But I appreciate your anger."

"I can't wait to go to the meeting today," Viv said.

"Why? It'll be so awkward. They don't even want us to know about it."

"Just to see the look on that guy's face," Viv said, slamming her locker shut. "This was an attempt to silence us, to rob us of the opportunity to be in that club and to go to San Diego! Our very presence will be an act of rebellion—our little way of sticking it to the man."

"I really don't like drama," Cam said. "I don't wanna deal with all that."

"Girl, you're already in it. It's too late. This email is proof."

Cam sighed. Vivian was right. Just Cam being in the class was enough to make Jeremy and his friends hate her.

"Let's go and be, like, awesome," Vivian said. "Let's run to the store at lunch and get doughnuts for the meeting."

"You want to bring a treat? After they left us off the list?"

"Yep!" she said. "Kill 'em with kindness. That's what my grandma used to say to my mom when boys put gum in her hair in elementary school."

"And how did that work out for your mom?"

"Not great. She cut her hair into a bob to make them stop."

Cam rolled her eyes as they took their seats in English.

"But you know what? Now she's a surgeon," Viv said. "So she showed them what they could do with their gum."

< br >

Cam felt queasy all afternoon. It was awkward enough to walk into class every day. How weird would it be to show up after Jeremy obviously uninvited them? She wasn't looking for a fight. If it weren't for Vivian, she probably wouldn't go.

After school the girls grabbed the stashed doughnuts from Cam's locker and went to the design lab, where the RoboSub team met. Jeremy was turning on the lights when they walked in.

"Oh, hi," he said, looking at them with scorn.

Matt, the copresident, gave them a small smile and waved. A cluster of boys shuffled in and took seats around the room.

"Hello, RoboSub friends," Vivian said.

Jackson shuffled in and slouched over his laptop in the back. Pretty much everyone else from Cam's CS class was there.

"Our invitation got lost in the mail." Viv glared at Jeremy. "But we wanted to contribute to the party." No sooner had she put down the box of doughnuts than the boys pounced on them.

The growing animosity between Jeremy and Vivian was palpable. Cam was proud of her friend for standing up to that jerk, but confrontation made her uncomfortable. Viv didn't have that problem.

"These seats free?" Viv asked rhetorically. She and Cam took seats at an empty workstation.

"Okay, so, welcome to RoboSub," Jeremy began. "Most of you were on the team last year, so you know how it goes. For new people, the bulk of our work happens in late spring and early summer. If that's a scheduling problem for anybody, let us know ASAP."

"You can still help the team!" Matt chimed in. "But you probably can't come to San Diego. We need to make sure the people who come work directly on the competition. Coding the sub, fixing hardware, speaking to the judges—"

Vivian's hand went up.

"Yes?" Matt asked.

"Are there scoring guidelines for the interviews?" she asked.

"Um, well, not for the interviews, no. But for the presentation there are."

"Excellent," Viv said, typing into her phone.

"Anyway, we'll ship the sub and parts ahead. We'll work until July, and then there's always a scramble on the last few days before the competition. That's for testing and making sure we can complete as many tasks as possible."

Viv's hand went up again. Jeremy stopped talking.

"When will we receive detailed information about the trip to San Diego? I want to give it to my parents."

"Our faculty advisor will send it out to everyone," Jeremy replied.

"Will that person use the same mailing list that was used to coordinate this meeting? Because that list was incomplete, as you know."

Matt gave a small smile that Jeremy erased with one glance. He cleared his throat. "I'll make sure Mr. Lenox has an updated list."

Great, Cam thought. *More Mr. Lenox.*

Both boys paused, waiting to see if Vivian had another interjection. She didn't.

"This year's theme is the sixties, so we need to come up with a video idea. Someone should take the lead on that," Jeremy said.

"We also need some new parts for the sub, so we'll need to make some new sponsor connections. The ones we had last year already agreed to cover our trip to San Diego," Matt added.

"Yeah, Matt's mom can't do all the sponsor coordination for him like last year," Jeremy said, nudging Matt.

Vivian's hand shot back up. "I'll volunteer to take that on."

"Really?" Matt said, looking relieved. "That would be so great. It was a ton of work, and you have to call all these strangers."

"Then it should probably be handled by a more experienced team member, in light of how difficult the task is," Jeremy said.

Matt glanced sideways at him. "Um, okay. Does anyone else want to do it?"

Crickets.

Vivian smiled and shrugged. "Guess it's me, then. Do I get a cool title?"

"Cool title?" Jeremy asked.

"I did some googling about this competition. Teams organize themselves in a variety of different ways, but it seems like there are four main roles. You need a business lead—that's the person who oversees sponsorship and marketing strategy. I'd like to run for that role."

"Run for it?" Matt asked.

"Yeah. How do you choose the leaders?"

"We just choose them," Jeremy said.

"Okay, so . . ." Vivian waited.

"I vote for Vivian," Cam said.

Matt nodded and smiled at Vivian. "Sounds good to me."

There was an awkward silence, and Jeremy looked at the other guys in the room. Most of them just munched on their snacks. No one seemed opposed to the idea.

"Fine," Jeremy said, teeth clenched. "You're the business lead. What's your name again?"

Vivian beamed. "Vivian Knix. K-N-I-X."

"Whatever," Jeremy responded, writing it down. "You can get last year's sponsor info from Matt."

"Great!" She leaned back in her chair and nudged Cam.

"Moving on," Jeremy said. Cam could tell he was trying to regain control. Vivian tended to pull attention—the director of student plays always used that phrase—and it could be a lot to adjust to. It was perfect for Cam, who preferred to blend into the background, but some people didn't respond all that positively.

"Everyone else, think about what you'd like to work on," Jeremy said. "At our next meeting, we'll have info sessions by team leads so you can learn more about the different roles and what work needs to be done."

"Right. So we basically need teams for electrical, software, and mechanical work," Matt continued. "Team leads are set for those already: Liam, Jack, and Spencer."

"Let's go!" Spencer said in that deep, loud voice boys did in the hallways. It made everyone laugh.

Cam didn't really get the joke. She also didn't know Spencer. He was a junior like Jeremy. Mechanical was definitely her team, so getting on Spencer's good side would be her next step.

Once the meeting wrapped up, she approached him as he packed up his bag. "Hey, I'm Cam," she said.

"Spencer," he said as he slung his bag over his shoulder.

"I'll probably want to be on the mechanical team," she said. *Probably?* More like absolutely. Why did she sound so unsure?

"Cool." He looked her up and down the same way most boys did when she interacted with them the first time. She felt exposed. Why was her body relevant to this conversation? To any conversation?

"So, do I need to know anything now?" she asked.

He shrugged and glanced toward the door where his friends were exiting the lab. "I'll bring stuff to the next meeting about it."

"Okay, thanks," she said. *Why am I thanking him? He told me nothing.*

He nodded and jogged after his friends, calling one of their names.

"So, first meeting down," Viv said, coming over to Cam and offering her a leftover doughnut.

"First meeting down," Cam repeated, selecting a chocolate glazed.

"All things considered, I think it went okay," Viv said.

"Mm-hmm," Cam mumbled through her mouthful of doughnut.

"I bet it really bothers Jeremy that I'm a lead now."

"Yeah, he didn't really hide that well. Hey," Cam said, pulling Vivian to the side of the hall. "Thanks for doing this with me. I really appreciate it."

"Girl, of course!" Vivian gushed. "And anyway, this'll be great for my transcript. A leadership role as a sophomore!"

"Yeah, but still. I know you probably wouldn't have signed up if it weren't for me."

"You're right," Vivian said. She looped an arm through Cam's and steered them toward their next class. "But I can't even count how many things I've done in my life because of you. If it weren't for you, I still wouldn't eat mac and cheese. And you know how much joy mac and cheese brings me."

Cam laughed. She had forgotten about her friend's aversion to melted cheese when they first met. "Yeah. I mean, when you put it that way, you're welcome."

< br >

The following morning before class started, Cam watched the door till Jackson arrived. He made eye contact with no one and went right to his seat, opening his laptop. She popped up from her desk and went to the empty one in front of his.

"Hey," she said, leaning over the top of his laptop.

He glanced up. "Hey."

"I just wanted to say thanks. For the Processing Foundation stuff."

He shrugged.

"I did know someone who needed some resources to get started with coding. And she found it really helpful."

He glanced up again. "Cool."

Feeling daring, she pushed the lid of his laptop slightly lower, forcing him to look up at her. "It really makes a difference to have someone offer help when you feel unwelcome somewhere," she said, looking straight at him.

She waited.

He blinked.

"I just wanted you to know that," she said. "And I saw you at RoboSub. Are you joining?

He shrugged and looked around. "I dunno. Maybe. It looked cool. My dad's always telling me I need to get more involved in stuff."

She smiled. "I'm glad you'll be there."

The bell rang, so she went back to her seat and got ready to take in more code.

```
(function imposter(){
    console.log("Chapter");
    console.log("Seven");
})();
```

Chapter Seven

Cam and Jackson needed to finish their project outline today. Normally Cam didn't cut it so close with assignment deadlines, but pinning Jackson down had proved difficult. He'd made it clear she shouldn't go to the attic, even though she suspected he spent most of his time there. That left them with lunch or after school, and she and Viv had planned on Aldo's for lunch. As sophomores, they could now go off campus. Jackson agreed to meet them there.

"It's fine. I don't mind third-wheeling," Vivian said, opening a bag of chips. "Academically, I mean." She wriggled her eyebrows suggestively at Cam.

The two friends had eaten lunch together every day for years. One time Viv took a trip with her family to Florida for a week in seventh grade, and Cam ate her lunch in the bathroom with her feet propped up on the door so the hall monitor wouldn't find her. It was harrowing.

Cam felt frazzled by her experience that day in class. She told Viv about it while they waited for Jackson.

When she got there, Jeremy was sitting in the desk behind hers. He had his feet on her chair, and they were dripping from the snow outside. His laptop was open, and he looked engrossed.

Mr. Lenox always showed up right before the bell, so there was no adult in the room. She had two options: choose a different seat and let him win, or make him move.

Taking a small breath to steady herself, she had cleared her throat. "Hey, can you move your feet? This is my seat."

He feigned surprise. "Oh, is it? Sorry. Forgot. My mom says I should sit closer to the front. Doesn't want my eyes to strain." He did not move.

"That's nice," Cam began, "but your wet feet are still on my seat."

"Oh, wow. Sorry," he said, smirking widely. He moved them. "Didn't even realize."

Cam had kept her tone civil. "Thanks," she said.

The seat was wet from his dirty shoes, but the Goldbergs were nothing if not loaded with tissues at all times (mostly due to allergies). She pulled some from her bag and wiped the seat clean.

"What an ass," Viv said after Cam finished the story. And then she gave Cam a chocolate chip cookie.

The two girls were chatting about the upcoming weekend when Jackson sidled up.

"Hey," he said. Cam was getting used to his physical appearance: always dressed in dark colors, usually black; hair a little too greasy; jeans and T-shirt way too baggy; limited eye contact.

"Hey, Jackson," Cam said, gesturing to the empty seat across from her. "Have a seat."

"Hey, Jackson, welcome to lunch," Viv said with a friendly look. He gained major points with her by helping Cam with coding stuff and by agreeing to be her partner. Viv was a fiercely loyal best friend.

Jackson seemed baffled by the attention. Mostly he ignored Viv, which Cam knew only further amused her. He mumbled a "hey" and gave them a slight nod.

"Okay. We have your sketches and the general outline of the game," Cam said, pulling up notes on her laptop.

"Mm-hmm," Jackson said, opening his own laptop. Cam knew by now he wasn't going into his notes. She also knew he needed a bit of a warm-up period before he would get talking.

"And we're going to add perks to raise money, like special weapons and . . . skins?" Cam asked. She wasn't totally familiar with all the terminology, but she was getting better.

"You're going to sell skin? Like customizations?" Viv asked.

"Skins means different looks for your character," Jackson replied.

"Oh, like the character creator!" Viv said, looking at Cam.

"Right. But, like, premade. Right, Jackson? Instead of just changing hair color or skin tone, it's a whole package of changes," Cam said.

"So, outfits?" Viv asked.

"Sure," he said. "There's a lot of variety. But yeah. It can be outfits."

"Ooh, fun. I'd spend money on that," Viv said, popping a chip into her mouth. "Do boys spend money on things like that? My cousin never wants to spend money on real clothes, but maybe he'd be down for fake clothes for his avatar or whatever."

Cam cringed inwardly. Vivian was revealing a lot—namely that they had never had a male friend before. Everything Cam knew about the opposite sex came from Netflix, YA novels, and TikTok. Sure, Cam could live vicariously through Viv's camp escapades, but it was an all-girls camp. They intermixed with the boys' camp only for special events a few times throughout the summer.

"Lots of people identify more with their avatars than they do with their real selves," Jackson said.

"Anyway, we'll charge for that stuff," Cam said. "Are you comfortable doing most of the artwork? I'm not particularly gifted in that area."

She felt bad, like most elements for the project depended on Jackson's skills. *That's not true*, she reminded herself. The original problem was her idea, and she'd done a lot of the research. Hopefully that was enough for now until she could improve her coding skills. Besides, she would do the storyboarding and interview some women to get more context for the game.

"Yeah. No big deal," he said.

"What if you made models of the weapons and stuff the characters have in the game?" Viv asked. Cam knew that Vivian could tell she was worried about not contributing enough. They knew each other so well.

"Like prototypes?" Cam asked.

"Sure! I think I know what that means," Viv said with a wink.

That idea wasn't half-bad. And it could show more nuance for their final presentation.

"Cool. I could do that!" Cam made a note. "So we have the idea, the problem, the way to raise money, and the work we can each do."

"Dope," Jackson said.

"So, Jackson," Viv said. "You have any winter carnival plans?" Winter carnival was like homecoming, but in winter. There was a big basketball game and a dance in the gym.

Cam looked up long enough to see Jackson flash Viv that familiar brief glance. "I don't go to stuff like that."

"Why not?" Viv asked. "We're going. You could come with us! Like, as a friends thing. Obviously."

Cam's head snapped up. *No, no, no,* she mouthed at Viv, who ignored her.

"No, thanks," he said. His keyboard went *click click click*.

"It would be fun! We mostly eat snacks and make fun of people who take it really seriously, and then we dance our faces off when the DJ plays a song we like. We watch movies after. We could watch something you like. *Star Wars*? *Star Trek*?"

"I like *Battlestar Galactica*."

"We could watch that!" Viv's face lit up.

"No, thanks," he said.

Her face fell. "Do you have other plans that night?"

"Yes," he said.

"Really?" Viv's surprise was clear, and Cam kicked her under the table.

"Yes. There's a tournament."

"Ooh. What kind?"

Jackson sat back and cracked his knuckles. Cam recognized that as the signal that his match had just ended. He looked at Vivian. *"Heroes of the Storm."*

Vivian nodded slowly. Cam hadn't heard of it before she started spending time with Jackson.

"Maybe you could come to the game with us and do your tournament thing after!"

"Nah. Thanks," he said, closing his laptop and gathering his bag.

"Oh! Can I get your number?" Cam asked. Probably bad timing, considering what Viv was trying to maneuver. Her friend gave her a look.

"I don't have a phone right now," Jackson said, prompting a further look from Viv. "I lost it, and my dad said he won't buy me a new one. Some responsibility bullshit lesson thing."

"How can we talk about the project?" Cam asked. "Email?"

"You could download the Battle.net app."

"The what?"

"It's this app that hosts all the Battle.net games. You know, like *HotS*."

Cam paused before asking what that was. She thought, *HotS* . . . Heroes of the Storm. *Ah. Like* CoD *for* Call of Duty. "Okay. But how will that help?"

"We can chat on it," he said, as if it were obvious. "And we can voice connect too, if you want."

"But would I have to be, like, playing a game?"

Jackson shook his head. "No. It's just an app that *hosts* the games. You'll see. I'll email you a link. You'll need a username."

"Um, okay. Cool. Bye!" Cam said as he waved and turned for the door.

Once he was out of earshot, she turned on Vivian. "What are you doing?"

Vivian laughed. "Come on. It would be so interesting to see him outside of school. And without his laptop! Oh god. You don't think he would, like, bring his laptop to the basketball game, do you?"

"Are you making fun of him?" Cam asked. Vivian had never been a mean girl, but Cam couldn't figure out where she was coming from right now. Jackson had been nice to Cam, and she didn't want to think her best friend would be mean to him.

"No! Cam, I swear I'm not." Viv sobered. "I just think he's a nice boy. A bit of a fixer-upper. But, you know, nice."

Vivian stared at her.

"No," Cam said, finally catching on.

"What? You two would be cute! He can be your coding mentor, and you can socialize him to survive the light of day!"

Cam crumpled up their garbage. "No way, Viv. We've talked about this. I am completely uninterested."

"Can you imagine how excited your dad would be? Jackson is so totally nonthreatening. He's every father's dream!"

"I can't hear you," Cam said, reaching over to throw out their trash.

"He has nice eyes underneath that overgrown hair. And he was kind to you when all those other guys were jerks. I think that's so sweet!"

"Then why don't *you* go out with him?"

Viv scrunched up her nose. "Not for me. Besides, I've recently decided to wait till college. Guys in high school are too emotionally stunted to handle me and all my realness."

Cam snorted. "Right. Well, me too."

"We'll see," Viv said, wriggling her eyebrows.

"We really won't, though," Cam said, walking away from the table.

"We'll see!" Viv called after her.

No chance, Cam thought.

```
(function imposter(){
    console.log("Chapter");
    console.log("Eight");
})();
```

Chapter Eight

At the next RoboSub meeting, leaders of each of the four teams (mechanical, electrical, software, and business) set up stations in the design lab so everyone could figure out which one they wanted to join. Cam tried to keep an open mind. Electrical could be just as interesting as mechanical, and a lot of the work she'd played around with at home combined the two.

Vivian had stressed all week about the meeting. Having just joined, she didn't know anything about the business team. Considering that last year the team had basically consisted of Matt's mom, Viv didn't have much to go on. But she'd made phone calls and signs with Cam's help and baked cupcakes the night before.

Each lead made a short presentation to the group. Viv nailed hers. The other leads were pretty vague and talked generally about how awesome their team was and how fun and chill it would be. Viv had an outline for sponsor recruitment, the competition presentation, and the design report.

After the speeches Cam felt the boys staring as she followed Viv to her table, but this time she knew why: food.

"Heeeeey. What's this over here?" Ryan asked as he reached past Vivian for a cupcake.

"Uh-uh!" Viv said, slapping his hand away.

"Ouch!" he said, sucking dramatically on his finger.

"I'm sorry. Did you take some sort of action to deserve this baked good?" Viv asked, hands on her hips.

"Umm..."

"Explain to me why you feel entitled to this cupcake that I spent three hours making and decorating last night."

"Uh."

"Yeah, no," Viv said, then spoke past him to the other boys. "No food for free! Anyone interested in a meaningful and genuine conversation about contributing to the business team is welcome to join me and partake of a delicious cupcake. Everybody else, hands off." She glared at Ryan.

Three boys approached immediately, standing a respectful distance from the cupcakes. They appeared to listen thoughtfully as Viv started talking. "Okay. So I've spent a *considerable* amount of time on the phone with Matt's mom—huge shout out to Mrs. O'Neal—and..."

Cam stepped out of earshot and went over to the table where Spencer slouched on a stool and looked at his phone.

"Hey," Cam said.

He looked up at her.

"I'm Cam," she said. "We met last week."

"Sure, I remember," Spencer said, still swiping.

"So could you tell me a bit about what the mechanical team does?"

He tabled his phone. "Yeah, it's pretty chill. We build the sub. Like the physical parts." He pointed at last year's sub on a shelf behind him. "So, like, once business gets the parts we need, we assemble them." His face brightened. "And we usually have good snacks. My mom hooks me up."

Cam nodded. "Who chooses which parts to buy?"

"What do you mean?"

"Like, who figures out the specs of the sub? How do you decide what you need?"

Spencer looked as if she'd asked the world's most ridiculous question. "We use what business gets."

Cam shifted her weight. Whenever she did a project, she did months of research first—reading about possible materials, how to use them, what tools she might need. The research was the bulk of the work. How could Spencer build a sub without doing research?

"How does business know what to get?"

Finally recognition showed up on Spencer's face. "Oh, right. We used the blueprint from Mr. Lenox."

"Wait, what? Mr. Lenox has a blueprint?" Cam had researched the RoboSub competition, and all the subs looked pretty different. She doubted there was some bank of blueprints that everyone pulled from. Teams posted videos about their design process, the research they did, the trial and error of the entire thing.

Spencer nodded. "We were just getting started last year, and we didn't have time to design the whole thing. So Mr. Lenox gave us a blueprint from some guy he knows, and we built it to those specifications."

"So then what will the mechanical team do exactly?"

"Make upgrades and stuff. Whatever comes up."

Cam had joined the club to get her hands dirty, not to dust off last year's model and eat Doritos with Spencer. "Okay, thanks," she said, moving away. Time to check out the electrical team.

The electrical table had some candy on it (more effort than Spencer had bothered to make). A couple boys spoke with Liam, a junior she recognized who wasn't in CS class.

"Hey, Cam," he said.

"Hey," she returned, trying to hide her surprise that he knew her name.

"You interested in electrical?"

"Oh, um, maybe. What does your team do?"

"It's the coolest part, I think," he said with a smile.

Cam felt her face get a little pink.

Liam continued, "We're responsible for making sure the electrical connections within the sub function properly. We also work with mechanical to make sure everything is watertight, since, you know, it's a sub."

Cam nodded. "Cool. So are you going to make changes this year? Spencer said there might not be much new building."

Liam gave her a knowing look and leaned in. She could smell his cologne—just a hint, not too much like those guys who caked it on after gym class. Her stomach did a little flip.

"Spencer's kinda lazy," Liam said. "I plan to do some revamping this year. I think we can clean up some inefficiencies. It will definitely take some rewiring. You ever soldered before?"

"Yep. I have," she said. She decided not to mention the Hanukkah candle that stood in for an iron.

"Cool. That's great. Last year we had to spend a lot of time getting it right. Some of the connections are really tight, so precision is important. You'll probably be really great for that, actually."

"Me?" she asked. It was the first time someone had said something positive about her presence in RoboSub, other than Vivian. "Why?"

"Small hands," he said.

"Oh, um, right." Cam became very conscious of her hands. What did she normally do with them while she was talking to people? Her arms kept moving. Crossing. Uncrossing. Tucking a strand of hair behind her ear. *Oh my god.* She finally put her hands flat in front of her.

"So I hope you'll join us," Liam said.

"Cool. Thanks," Cam said, and she scurried to the safety of Vivian's table.

"Hey, friend!" Viv greeted her. "You check everything out?"

No, actually. Cam avoided the software table where Jeremy was showing off the code he'd worked on the year before. Most of the other guys clustered around him.

"I checked out everything of interest," Cam said.

"Here. Have a cupcake and talk to me about business," Viv said, offering the almost-empty plate.

Then Matt came over. "Hey, Vivian, thanks for taking on all this stuff," he said. "I was supposed to do it last year, but I didn't really get it. My mom saved us all by jumping in."

"Yeah. Your mom is great," Viv said. "We chatted. Solid lady, knows her stuff. She went to Wharton!"

"Yeah, she's kind of a big deal at her work," Matt said. "I don't really know what she does."

"She's a VP of sales at Procter & Gamble," Viv said.

"Yeah. We always get free lotion and stuff," Matt said with a laugh.

Viv just looked at him.

"So thanks for doing this for us," Matt said, before sliding back to Jeremy's station.

Vivian turned to Cam. "How could he not know that his mom's job is a huge deal?"

Cam laughed. "Seriously."

Vivian threw up her hands. "How does no one care about industry? It's only, like, the bedrock of our entire economy. It's the way we get everything we have, produce everything we make, sell everything we produce. Like, hello?" She dug into a cupcake, and then wiped frosting from the tip of her nose. "Businesspeople are so undervalued."

Cam had heard Viv's business-is-everything rant before, so she just nodded and nibbled her cupcake.

Things began to wind down. Cam was helping Vivian pack up her supplies when Jeremy came over.

"Vivian, the club members would appreciate if you would bring cupcakes again," he said, all formal and brusque.

"Excuse me?" Viv said.

"The club members—"

"I heard your words," Viv said, cutting him off. "Are you telling me to bring baked goods to the next meeting?"

He sighed and rolled his eyes. "I'm not telling—"

"Because I *know* you're not asking one of your two female members to bake snacks for you, like your own personal nanny or something."

Wow, Cam thought. *How is she so brave?*

"Some of the guys just said they like having baked snacks," he said.

Vivian hiked her bag onto her shoulder and took a step closer to him. "Then I suggest you learn to bake, Jeremy. Because we're not friends, you and me. And you know what? I don't like how you talk to my bestie. So this baked goods problem sounds like a personal one to me." With that she made for the door, Cam hot on her heels.

"That was awesome," Cam said as they entered the hallway.

Vivian only winked.

< br >

Mr. Lenox shared his screen as he wrote out some code. The more Cam studied, the more she could actually follow as he did this. Most of the class chatted about other things. The occasional snicker or scoff came from behind her, but that could be about anything. The week before, she kept hearing snippets of conversation about the Ohio University Bobcats.

But Cam always paid close attention in class, absorbing whatever she could. Today Mr. Lenox was working with vectors, and Cam had just watched some online classes about how to manipulate vectors in p5. Mr. Lenox had written out the code.

```
1   function setup() {
2     createCanvas(640, 360);
3     w = new Walker ();
4   }
5
6   function draw() {
7     background(51);
8     w.update();
9     w.display();
10  }
11
12
13  function Walker() {
14    this.pos = createVector(width/2, height/2);
15    this.vel = createVector(0,0);
16    this.acc = p5.Vector.fromAngle(random(0,TWO_PI))
17    this.acc.setMag(0.2);
18
19    this.update = function(){
20      this.acc.rotate(0.1);
21      this.vel.add(this.acc);
22      this.pos.add(this.vel);
23    }
24
25    this.display = function(){
26      fill(255);
27      ellipse(this.pos.x, this.pos.y, 48, 48)
28    }
29  }
```

The code created a large dot that rotated in big lazy circles as it twirled off the screen. "How can I make the movement tighter and faster?" Mr. Lenox asked the class.

No one responded, and Cam knew the answer. Before she could overthink it, she let her hand go up.

"Ms. Goldberg?"

"Adjust the acceleration of the rotation?" Why did she phrase it as a question? It was the correct answer. "If you make it accelerate faster, the circles will tighten as well."

Snickering came from behind her.

"Please refer to the line specifically, Ms. Goldberg."

"Right," she said. "Line twenty. You could change that to a larger decimal, like point five."

"Let's see," Mr. Lenox said. He liked to try their solutions live in class, so the class could debug together. He updated the code with her solution.

```
20      this.acc.rotate(0.5);
```

The dot spun tightly now, and its movement looked more like a vibration than an ambling spin off the canvas. Exactly as she thought.

"Well done," Mr. Lenox said. Her first praise from him. "Now, Mr. Woburn?"

He caught Jeremy off guard. "Yep," Jeremy responded, even though he clearly hadn't been paying attention. He squinted up at the screen.

"Explain Ms. Goldberg's solution."

There was a pause. "Um . . ." Cam had said why the solution worked, but Jeremy hadn't been listening.

"Uh, it increases the velocity?" he said. It was an okay guess—the function for velocity was up on the screen. But it was wrong.

"Mr. Woburn, it's surprising that an advanced member of our class would be unable to answer that question. Mr. Wentworth."

"Yep?" Jackson's eyes did not leave his screen.

"The same question."

"Acceleration literally is the rate of change in velocity. It's like Cam said. Increased acceleration is the result of either an increase in velocity or a decrease in time. If we increase acceleration with no change in time, velocity must increase."

The room was shocked into silence. *Whoa. Jackson pays more attention than he lets on*, Cam thought.

Jackson shrugged. "Basic physics."

"That's correct, Mr. Wentworth," Mr. Lenox said, thinly veiling his own surprise. "The rest of you would do well to brush up on your ninth-grade physics."

Cam slumped down in her desk and tried to hide her grin.

< br >

Since Viv was working with her DECA team on their ICDC entries that Saturday, Cam played with code in the p5 editor until her eyes crossed.

"Hey, Cam, wanna watch this TED Talk I found?" her dad asked after rapping on the door.

She took our her AirPods. "About what?"

"It's by the woman who founded that organization I told you about, Girls Who Code," he said. "Reshma Saujani."

"Sure. I could use a break." She unfolded herself from the bed and followed him downstairs.

Her mom was on the couch looking sort of emotional. *What's going on?* Cam thought.

When her dad hit play, Cam saw the title: *Teach Girls Bravery, Not Perfection.*

The talk opened with Reshma discussing her run for Congress. "It was the first time in my entire life that I had done something that was truly brave, where I didn't worry about being perfect," Reshma said.

She talked about how girls are raised to be nice and play it safe, while boys are conditioned to take risks and not worry about the consequences. This difference in socialization caused what Reshma called "the bravery deficit," which in turn led to women being underrepresented in STEM, among other things.

Cam was hooked.

"At the fifth-grade level," Reshma said, "girls routinely outperform boys in every subject, including math and science."

Cam knew that from her research.

"So, it's not a question of ability," Reshma went on.

Cam knew that in her heart.

She also knew that CS class was a daily misery at first, despite how interested she was in the content. On a good day her classmates pretended like she didn't exist. On less-good days she heard them whisper about her.

I've thought about quitting, she thought. *If it weren't for Viv, maybe I would've.*

Instead she'd dug in and worked hard. Her weekends and evenings were filled with studying code, and it felt like things were starting to click. Giving up was not on the table. The more Cam learned and read about women in the industry, the more her determination grew.

"It turns out that our girls are *really* good at coding," Reshma said. "But it's not enough just to teach them to code." She talked about a professor at Columbia who taught Java. During office hours, the boys came in to say something was wrong with their code. The girls said something was wrong with them or their work.

Cam felt tears in her eyes, and a tightness in her throat. Her mom put a hand over Cam's.

Reshma talked about women afraid to ask questions because they thought they were the only ones who didn't understand.

About the girls in her organization who were coding; who had worked past their fear of failure and embraced imperfection; who had invented amazing things—including a game called *Tampon Run* to dispel period stigma. Other girls like Cam were out there, putting in the work outside of school, figuring out how to make things—things they cared about that only they could make.

"When we teach girls to be imperfect, and we help them leverage it, we will build a movement of young women who are brave, and who will build a better world—for themselves, and for each and every one of us," Reshma said.

The video ended, and her father looked at Cam. "So what did you think?"

Cam looked down at her hands and focused on breathing evenly. The talk made her want to cry. It was comforting to know she wasn't alone—that girls and women like her were everywhere and interested in contributing and making things. But they faced the same issues as in Cam's little town in Ohio. In every town, girls like her got squashed by other people's expectations. By stereotypes and prejudice. By jerks like Jeremy.

"I think I know what she means about raising girls to be perfect," Mom said. "Your dad and I worry about that with you. Your abuela can be pretty demanding. Have I ever talked to you about that?"

Cam shook her head. "No. But I see that sometimes when she comes to visit. She always makes little comments about what you cook and stuff."

One year at the Passover seder, there'd been a very tense conversation about the right kind of oil to fry latkes. It was one of the few times Cam was told to leave the room so the adults could talk.

"And I get what she means in the video. I see it at school. Girls don't want to do things they struggle with, or they're afraid of making a mistake in front of everyone." *I've done it too.*

"I struggled with that when I was your age," Mom said, giving Cam's hands a squeeze. "I had to be so perfect for abuela, because I was here in the States with all these opportunities she didn't have when she was younger. It was a lot of pressure to make the most of everything. To be the best and to never mess up."

Cam's mother paused, her gaze drifting absently to the TV. She took a deep breath and turned back to Cam. "I don't want you to feel that. Who knows what I would have tried if I'd been free to."

Dad turned toward Cam. "Your mom and I see how hard you work. And we're proud of you. You're learning a new thing, and we know that can be really hard."

Cam nodded, tears welling again. Compliments always made her tear up.

"And you might not get it right the first time or the second time," Mom said.

"But hey, can you do it?" Dad asked.

This phrase was a tradition in their family. When Cam was little she had a book called *From Head to Toe*, by Eric Carle. The book asked the same question over and over: "Can you do it?" Cam's parents asked the question, and Cam always said the next line: "I can do it!" It became a mantra as Cam got older, especially whenever she tried a new thing.

A tear rolled down her cheek as she laughed. "Yeah. I can do it."

Her father gave her a hug, and she felt her mom join from the other side. "We know you can," Dad said.

Back in her room, Cam sent Reshma's TED Talk to Vivian. Fifteen minutes later, Viv texted back **YAS girl** with a GIF of a cat twerking. Cam rolled back on her bed laughing, then stared at her star-plastered ceiling.

Maybe she wasn't so alone in this after all. As she looked up at the plastic stars that had faded as she'd gotten older, images of all the girls out there—girls like her—flashed through her mind. They manifested as their digital avatars, like on Girls Who Code Girls. They represented the thousands—maybe millions—of girls around the world from different cultures and perspectives. Snippets of code danced across the stars and customized their different features: short, tall, every shape, every skin tone, every religion, nonbinary, neurodivergent. Each adjustment to the code changed another feature and created another unique girl. Created an example for the girls who would come next, so they could see themselves in the digital world in a way Cam never did. So they would belong.

We can do it.

```
(function imposter(){
    console.log("Chapter");
    console.log("Nine");
})();
```

Chapter Nine

By the following RoboSub meeting, Cam had decided to join the electrical team. Learning as much as possible as fast as possible was her top priority.

"Nice. This is a good crew!" Liam said.

The electrical team had four people, which tied it with software. Mechanical had three. Unfortunately Viv was the sole member of the business team, but she didn't seem to mind. Jackson was sitting with Spencer and the mechanical team.

"So I thought we could spend today getting familiar with the electrical network in the sub," Liam said. "Since you're all new, getting to know where we've already been seems like a good place to start. Has anybody worked with a self-contained machine like this before?"

One other person, Jeff, said he'd done a little wiring on his family's computer.

"Cool!" Liam said.

Nobody else shared anything, so Liam brought the sub over to their table and removed the outer shell. It looked like a mess of cables, boards, and pieces Cam didn't recognize—like a heavy hovercraft. And it seemed like it could definitely be more organized.

Cam took extensive notes while Liam explained the different parts and connections. No one else took notes, but Cam brushed that off.

"Any questions?" Liam asked.

Cam glanced around. The boys all looked down or away. She raised her hand.

"You don't have to raise your hand," Liam said with a grin. "You can just ask."

"Oh, cool," Cam said. Her face got hot. "I was wondering how flexible this design is. Like, how much can we change it?"

"Oh, so you think we did a bad job?" he joked.

She laughed.

"We were really just stabbing in the dark last year. It was the first time we'd ever done this, so we sort of made it up, to be honest. We had blueprints to work from, but that was mostly for the hardware team. I think we could do a lot better this year, especially with some new brains." Liam made eye contact with Cam the whole time he spoke.

"Cool," Cam said, looking away and pretending to write something in her notebook.

"Any other questions?" Liam looked around. "No? Then let's get to work."

< br >

Jackson and Cam met up at Aldo's again to work on their project. They'd showed up so much recently that the manager gave them the stink eye if they didn't buy more stuff after an hour or so. Luckily Jackson had an insatiable appetite for Nerds Ropes.

"Here are the final characters," Jackson said. For someone who seemed totally checked out, he'd done a lot of work since their last meeting. Cam's research was nearly done as well, and their project presentation wasn't until May. About three months away.

"These look so great!" Cam said. She flashed the superhero businesswoman at Vivian. Viv had been working nonstop on her project submission for the ICDC. It was hard to get her attention, but Jackson's sketches made her perk up.

"Oooh. I love her belt," Viv gushed. "Very functional, yet flattering."

"Thanks," Jackson said, turning slightly pink.

Cam had learned that this style of art was called thick-line animation because it featured thick black lines around all the interactive characters and objects. Jackson said the style made it easier for players to know what they could or could not manipulate in the game.

"So we need some people to record the character phrases, and we need a big-boss character. I was thinking. Since we're doing only one level for the presentation, we could make the boss an exaggerated, larger version of the Blockheads," Jackson said.

They had decided to call the male Goomba-like characters Blockheads. It was silly enough to get the point across but not be taken too seriously. And it was the most G-rated, school-appropriate name they could come up with. Jackson made their heads more blocky to reflect the name and keep the tone goofy.

"Maybe if we expand the game, we could add Knuckleheads and Boneheads," Cam said.

"Could there be different versions of the girls you can play?" Viv said.

"Like different skins? Or different characters with different abilities?" Jackson asked.

"Um. Either one?" Viv said.

Jackson nodded. "Skin options would be pretty easy. I'd just need to do different drawings. Adding more characters could be an area of expansion for the future. We should mention that in our presentation." He said the last part to Cam, and she made a note.

"Cool. So I'll get access to the school's Unity account, and we can start building the code next week," Jackson said.

"What's Unity?" Vivian asked.

"A game engine," he replied.

"What's a game engine?" Viv smiled.

"Like, the platform you make a game on," Cam offered.

"Cool," Viv replied with a shrug.

"I'll be online a lot this weekend if you wanna chat or voice while we work," Jackson said, saving his work and getting ready to leave. "Did you activate your Battle.net?"

Cam cringed. "Not yet. I'll do it this weekend."

He shrugged. "Cool. Just let me know your handle." He waved and left.

As soon as he was gone, Viv said, "Oh my god. What is your username going to be? We have to think of an awesome one."

"I don't know. I'll probably just use my Instagram handle or something."

"No!" Vivian shouted. "And risk people making the connection between this battleland thing and your real self?"

Cam laughed. "Well, what do you suggest?"

"Hmmmm." Viv thought for a few moments. "This will be a weekend brainstorm project. I can tell."

< br >

Cam and Viv sipped hot chocolate in the middle of the bleachers. Not at the top with the band kids and not at the bottom with the school-spirit kids. Middle of the road. The basketball game was not going well, and Viv was driving Cam crazy with ideas for a Battle.net name.

"How about something female sounding. LadyBeast?"

Cam shook her head. "Guys get pretty annoying if they realize you're a female player."

"Why is that not surprising?" Viv said, rolling her eyes. "What about something more mysterious, like MsNomer."

"Misnomer? Like the word?"

"No, like *Miss Nomer*. Like a play on the word but with *Ms* instead of *Miss*. A nod to the fact that you're a girl. It's a mysterious word that means an inaccurate name. And it could be shorthand for the actual word, so not necessarily a girl name, you know?"

"Wow. Have you studied for the SAT already?"

"No. But I did an excellent job on my PSAT. Thank you for noticing!"

Cam thought about the name. "What if it had a *g*. Like a garden gnome."

"Love it."

Cam opened the account page and typed in MsGnomer. "It's available!"

"Yassssssss!"

"Okay, I did it," Cam said. She put the number Jackson had given her in the Add a Friend menu. A few seconds later he accepted her request.

"Ooh, look. I can see what my friends are doing," Cam said. There was text under Jackson's battle tag—InvaderJim—that said "Playing Storm League."

"What does that mean?" Viv asked.

"I'm not sure."

"Well, are you going to say something to him?"

"Nah. Let's leave him alone. He probably won't respond if he's playing ranked anyway."

A group of boys entered the gym and lingered in the doorway, drawing Cam's attention.

"Jeremy," Viv said, tipping her head in that direction.

It was a big game, so Cam wasn't surprised to see him. She was about to turn her attention back to the game when one of the other guys caught her eye—Liam. He smiled and waved. She started to smile and wave back, but Jeremy turned to see who Liam waved at, caught Cam's eye, and shot her a glare.

Viv took a discreet sip of cocoa. "That Liam's kinda cute..."

Cam rolled her eyes. "He's a junior."

"So? What's a year? Jay-Z is twelve years older than Beyoncé."

Sneaking a peek from the corner of her eye, Cam saw Liam, now messing around with the other guys in the bleachers. He had a sort of kindness about him. Since he'd moved to town in middle school, he hadn't seen Cam go through her *Blue's Clues* phase. His arrival in eighth grade was big news (it was rare they had new kids in the mix). She didn't know much about him, though, because the grades didn't intermingle much, and he moved on to high school the next year.

Maybe Viv is right—he is kinda cute, Cam thought. As if he could hear her, he glanced over in her direction again, causing her to snap her eyes back to her phone. She was near the door, so he was probably just looking for a friend.

Or maybe he was looking in her direction for another reason entirely.

< br >

After Vivian left from their sleepover the next morning, Cam downloaded the Battle.net app on her laptop and started a chat with Jackson, who was online again. Or maybe still.

MsGnomer: Hi! It's Cam. From school.
InvaderJim: hi

InvaderJim: cool name
MsGnomer: Thanks!
MsGnomer: Could you send me the link for Unity?
InvaderJim: unity.com
MsGnomer: Ha, oh, duh
InvaderJim: I'll set up a collab for us
InvaderJim: You should play around to get the hang of it
MsGnomer: Okay!

Cam followed the directions on the website, but the download took forever, so she had time to kill. Opening a new document, she started to outline her plan for a proposed Girls Who Code club at school. The programs offered by Girls Who Code in the summer were interesting, but Cam wanted something during the school year. A place at MacArthur High School for girls like her who wanted to build things. Or even just a place for girls who might be into making to explore various interests. Access to the design lab was so limited, and most of her teachers didn't use it. If it weren't for CS class and RoboSub, she probably still wouldn't have been in there. In addition to donating funds to Girls Who Code national, their CS project could support a local club at school.

She wasn't sure about the faculty advisor. The club had to be approved first anyway. What she needed now was a description of the club for their project materials. She started typing, then stared out her window for a few minutes. Her parents were clearing off the porch, still a mess from winter. Her father was showing her mother a new tool he'd bought, and her mother looked skeptical. Cam typed more.

> The mission of Girls Who Code (GWC) at MacArthur is to expose more people to engineering and design and to facilitate more access to the tools and resources in

the design lab. Despite its name, GWC encourages people of all genders to be part of the club, as long as they support providing girls with safe, girl-focused spaces.

She pulled up the Unity installer and saw that it was only at 56.2 percent. Perfect timing to go on a snack hunt.

Cam's parents found her digging in the fridge a few minutes later.

"Ah, the prodigal daughter emerges from her lair for sustenance," Dad said.

"Very funny," Cam replied, emerging with her arms full.

"Nena, why not make some real lunch instead?" Mom asked.

"Lunch is a social construct," Cam replied. "It's all just food entering my belly whenever I need more of it. Which is basically all the time."

Her parents both laughed.

"Well, I'm going to make a salad," her dad said. "Would anyone like some?"

Her mother said yes, but Cam glanced down at her haul—two string cheeses, a chocolate-milk box, some loose deli meat, and a chicken nugget from two dinners ago.

"Nope," she said. "I'm good here."

"How are you progressing with your project?" her mom asked.

"I think it's going well. I'm waiting for Unity to download so I can start working on the game with Jackson. I already did the research, and I'm working on the proposal for the solution now."

"What's Unity?" her mom asked.

Cam thought for a second about the best way to explain. "You know how you use, like, Microsoft Word to make documents?"

"Of course," her mom said. "Or Google Docs."

"Right," Cam said. "Unity is like that, but for making games. So it's like the platform you make the game on. It's called a game engine."

"Ooooh. Look at our Cameron learning so much about game engines and platforms," Mom teased, poking at Cam as she dodged away.

"What are other people doing for their projects?" Dad asked.

Cam rolled her eyes. None of the other projects sounded like solutions to real problems. She filled in her parents. Two boys were working on an app that reminds you to do homework and chores—a glorified calendar—because they could never remember those things. Jeremy and Matt were building something to make it easier to order food with your friends. Cam didn't consider splitting a pizza to be a systemic problem in need of an urgent solution.

"Those sound . . . interesting," her mom said. "Not like yours, though." She paused, exchanging a look with Cam's dad. "I wonder if your topic is a little . . . ambitious for this project."

Her dad cringed.

Her mom clarified, "Well I don't mean *ambitious*—that's not the right word. It's maybe too . . ."

"Broad?" her dad tried.

Cam narrowed her eyes at him, and he shrugged.

"The more I read about this stuff, the more I realize that this is a big deal," Cam said. "A real problem that needs solving. And that is the assignment."

"It doesn't need to be your problem, nena. Does it?" Mom tried. "I mean, the food-sharing thing. That's easy. Just make an app that fixes it—there's not so much gray area."

"What do you mean?" Cam tried not to crush her food in annoyance.

Her mother wiped something on the counter. "I just wonder if it's worth all this trouble. You could still be interested in coding and making without your whole project depending on it. I worry it creates a lot of stress for you."

"What trouble?"

"Gabi . . ." Cam's dad said, like a warning.

What is going on? Cam thought. *They're always on the same page.*

"The way you speak about this class. It doesn't seem like a very good experience," her mom said. "And your research makes this seem like a big issue—much bigger than a school project can solve."

"So, what? You think I shouldn't have started this project?"

Her parents looked at each other.

"Do you think I shouldn't have taken the class?"

"Ay, I don't know. I don't think I like it for you, that's all," her mom said. "It seems Vivian is having a better time with her sculpture class. It calms her. This course causes you stress. You work all the time, and for what?"

"Because I want to do this with the rest of my life, Mom!"

"But it doesn't seem like a place for women!"

The silence that followed was palpable. *Not a place for women?* Dad's eyes ping-ponged between the two of them. Cam and her mom stared at each other. Mom looked pained, but Cam didn't understand why.

"Well, I didn't ask you," Cam said, whirling away. Then she turned back. "And by the way, I think every place is a place for women. That's kind of the whole point."

As she stormed back to her room, Cam's mind raced. This was not her mother: champion of women, fighter for women's rights. Her mother always encouraged Cam to try new things, to take chances, to explore. How could she possibly think that Cam should give up her dream because the field was predominantly men? Wasn't that all the more reason to fight? To change it? Cam's parents always told her how smart she was and how she could study and learn anything. Success wasn't about talent; it was about hard work. Was her mother prejudiced against women in technical fields?

Another hurdle, and this one in her own house. Cam felt overwhelmed, but determined to keep going—she'd come this far and put up with this much. She was going to crush this project, crush RoboSub, and prove everyone wrong.

A soft knock came at her door. She knew it would be Mom. They rarely fought, and her parents were talkers—always wanting to rehash what went wrong and figure out how to make it better. Cam wasn't like that. Sometimes she just needed to be mad.

Her mom knocked one more time. "Nena, can I come in? I didn't mean what I said. Those weren't the right words."

Cam closed her eyes and sighed. She was in no mood, but she gave in. "Fine, come in."

Her mother looked like a dog with its tail between its legs. Approaching the bed, Mom looked at Cam for permission to sit down. Cam nodded.

"Cam. What I said downstairs . . . that came out wrong. Of course I think you can and should do anything you set your heart and mind to. I really do," she started.

Cam stared at her hands.

"I think I just meant that . . . it seems harder. To choose this path. And I've seen people choose a hard road before. It can change you." Mom paused and looked at the wall. "We should talk about Alexendra."

Cam perked up. *Finally*.

"My cousin. She lives with the Rodriguez side of the family in Panama City," Mom began. "She's close to my age actually—we're just two years apart."

Cam nodded. She'd been to Panama a few years earlier, but she didn't recall meeting an Alexendra.

"She was very talented in school. Gifted, people said. She and I used to compete for the best grades," Mom said with a little laugh. "Anyway, her parents saved up to send her to school in the US, like me. She went to Barnard, the women's college in New York City?"

Cam nodded. She knew the sister school to Columbia on the Upper West Side. Her parents mentioned it from time to time when they recounted their college days.

Mom continued. "She wanted to study law. To be a lawyer in America and then one day open a practice back in Panama. She actually went to NYU as well, but for law school, so we weren't there at the same time. It was very hard work. We didn't hear much from her during those years. When she finished, she got a job at a big law firm in Manhattan. She was *so* excited. Your dad and I went to a party to celebrate with her. She was glowing. The salaries at these firms are so large . . . more money than her family had saved up for all four years of college, just for one year of working. We all felt that she'd realized her dream."

Okay, Cam thought. *What does this story have to do with me?*

Her mom took a deep breath. "And then the next thing we knew . . . only a few months later . . . she quit. She said she couldn't do it anymore, and she was going back home to Panama."

"What?" Cam said, breaking her silence. "Why would she do that?"

Her mother's brow furrowed. "I went to help her pack. She was so different from her usual self. She looked . . . tired. Drained. But it was more than that. Her brightness had dimmed. When I asked her why she quit, she would only say that she'd been wrong to think someone like her could make a name for herself in big law. She seemed so resigned and defeated." Mom shrugged. "I never got the details. She wouldn't share them then, and it's not something the family talks about now."

"What is she doing now?" Cam asked.

"She got married a few years later and had children quickly after that. Her husband manages properties in Panama and she keeps the books. Last I heard, she was happy with that."

Cam nodded. There was nothing wrong with choosing to have children and raise them. Her parents talked about that a lot. When Cam was born, it was her father who took a long parental leave to be home with her. But this story felt different.

"I can still picture her face when I showed up to help her move. Her passion, her fire, the girl I'd known my whole life—I couldn't see her." A soft tear trickled down Mom's face. Brushing it away, she turned to Cam. "These things you tell me about women in engineering. They remind me of what Alexendra shared with me about law school. Foolish men who made her feel small, refused to share notes with her, cut her off in class, left her out of study groups. I can only assume she continued to struggle with that behavior at work too. It broke her, I think."

Mom took Cam's hands and looked straight at her. "I don't want it to break you."

"Mom—" Cam began.

"Let me finish. I don't mean to say that I think it *will* break you, or that you can't handle it, or that you shouldn't fight for it," Mom went on, more tears in her eyes now. "I think that you can do all that. But I don't want you to have to deal with that. If you didn't do this, you wouldn't have to. I don't know if that makes any sense."

Cam nodded, her own eyes getting wet. "It does."

Mom sniffled and adjusted on the bed. "I know you. You'll do what is the right next thing for you in your heart. And that is exactly what Papa and I want for you," she said. "But I wish it didn't come with this nonsense. What happened with Alexendra was twenty years ago. Yet here's my daughter dealing with the same mierda. It saddens me very much."

Cam squeezed her mom's hands. "I get that," she said. "I really do." She took a breath. "What happened to Alexendra... that's exactly the kind of story that makes me want to do this more, you know? She deserved better. She deserved to have the career she wanted, to succeed in New York, to open her own practice in Panama. She's not the only one this has happened to. Her story is so, so common. And you know what, Mom?"

"What?"

"It pisses me off."

Her mother laughed, and Cam laughed with her.

"Every time I hear a story like this, it makes me want to keep going. Not even for me. For them. For the Alexendras." Cam shrugged. She didn't know how else to say it. "And if I can make some tiny step forward, then that's enough for now."

Her mom beamed. "I'm so proud of you, nena. Sometimes this might be hard for me, but I'm going to try. And I'm sorry, okay?"

Cam hugged her. "It's okay, Mom. I love you."

"I love you too."

< br >

Later that evening, Cam pulled up Battle.net and saw Jackson was still online. She wondered if he ever logged off.

> MsGnomer: Unity is cool!
> InvaderJim: I know right
> MsGnomer: I see how to add sprites and objects but how do we get everything set up initially?
> InvaderJim: in the collab
> InvaderJim: already did the wallpaper and we have the sprites. Need weapons next.
> MsGnomer: Cool and then I can start prototyping. Will she fight with hands too?

InvaderJim: It makes sense to start with hands, but cooler if she can pick up items and use them and unlock cool weapons and stuff
MsGnomer: Like what?
InvaderJim: I don't know, a stapler or something low-level. Office stuff
MsGnomer: Maybe headphones, phone charger, coffee cup
InvaderJim: We need a range. Really powerful ones and some less
MsGnomer: maybe message from a friend as a superpower boost?
InvaderJim: Like a note?
MsGnomer: Like a text. Maybe it turns phone into a weapon?
InvaderJim: Cool, yeah, it could morph it into a weapon
InvaderJim: will work on that
MsGnomer: Great!

Cam signed off and got to work on her paper. Then she studied for her upcoming math test. She wasn't sure how she could take on any more work than she had. Once RoboSub started in earnest, she might be in trouble.

```
(function imposter(){
    console.log("Chapter");
    console.log("Ten");
})();
```

Chapter Ten

A couple weeks later, Cam and Viv were three hours into a Netflix binge. Viv's parents were at some event, so the girls had the house to themselves. When the fourth episode ended, Viv turned off the TV and opened her laptop. "Let's see if Jackson is online," she said.

"Why?" Cam asked. She already talked plenty to Jackson for their project.

"I'm curious about this *HotS* game he's always playing. Have you ever tried it?"

"Not yet," Cam said.

"Let's make a name for me on Battle.net. What should it be?" The girls brainstormed a few options. WonderWoman was taken. So were RBG4Life and Ginsburg.

"I got it!" Viv said. She typed in a screenname.

"PrezRoslin?" Cam said.

"It's a *Battlestar Galactica* thing."

"You know *Battlestar Galactica* things?"

"Yeah, I've watched a little of it." Viv blushed slightly.

Viv searched for Jackson's battle tag. "He's on!" she screeched. She opened a chat.

PrezRoslin: hey

There was a pause.

InvaderJim: hey.

InvaderJim: cool battle tag

Viv squealed. "See? He gets it. Let's find out what he's up to."

"I don't understand what we're doing," Cam said.

"This is like a window into Jackson's secret world!"

"Aren't you going to tell him who you are?"

"And spoil the fun of anonymity? Why?" Viv looked confused.

A new message from Jackson popped up.

InvaderJim: qm?

"Omigod. What does that mean?" Viv asked.

"How should I know? I don't play these games."

"Quick, ask Siri! Google it!"

Cam googled "Heroes of the Storm qm" and scanned the results. "Quick match," she reported. "It's a type of game, I guess?"

"Is he asking if we want to play one?"

"I think so," Cam said.

"Omigod. He's going to realize we don't know how to play! We can't!"

"Let's just tell him we don't know how."

PrezRoslin: it's my first time

Viv giggled at her own cleverness.

InvaderJim: no prob, want to learn?

"Awww. He's so nice. Look at him being nice as his online persona."

Before they could respond, another window popped up.

MrBigCluck: you a girl?

"Don't respond to that," Cam said, but Viv typed back anyway.

PrezRoslin: Yes, why?
MrBigCluck: lol girls are trash at HotS why are you on here?
PrezRoslin: Excuse me? The game is online, it only requires my ability to use a computer.
MrBigCluck: W/e lez. I bet you just play bc your bf does.

"What the hell? Who is this person?" Viv asked.

"Let's just block him," Cam replied.

"But why would he do that? This is, like, where they do most of their socializing. Wouldn't this be a great place to meet someone with mutual interests? They're depriving themselves of a meaningful opportunity!"

"I doubt they think that hard about it," Cam replied. "Report him, and maybe the admins will do something."

Viv reported MrBigCluck. A notification popped up on the screen. InvaderJim invited them to a quick match.

"Should we do it?" Viv asked.

Cam shrugged. "Why not?"

An hour later the girls had taken turns playing four quick-match games, all of which ended quickly. They learned the game was played in teams of five, and their teammates (besides Jackson) weren't very happy with how often they died. MrBigCluck wasn't the only one to figure out Vivian's gender from her battle tag, so the comments they received were not particularly kind.

InvaderJim: You can mute those people if you want.

"Oh! Everyone can see the messages. Muting is perfect," Vivian said, clicking on some players.

They were about to start a new game when they heard the front door open and slam shut.

"I told you I didn't want to go to that stupid bar!" Vivian's mom shouted.

Viv froze, her face ashen.

"Would it kill you to get out and spend time with my friends for once?" Mr. Knix shouted back.

They heard the clatter of his keys landing somewhere hard.

"Why? So I can listen to lazy assholes talk about football and trucks?"

Cam put a hand on Viv's shoulder and felt her friend's rapid breathing.

"I bet you'd just love for me to go alone, so you could go meet up with your—"

"Richard! We've talked about this. I'm not steppin' out on you."

"That's a lie!"

"Hey. Let's go," Cam said, gently closing Viv's laptop.

Her friend was totally frozen, clutching the blanket beneath them. Cam grabbed a tote bag hanging from the door and pulled some clothes from Viv's drawers.

"Come on," she said, taking Viv's hand. "Come sleep over. You can drive us." Viv got her license over winter break.

Viv had tears in her eyes. "They'll see us," she said quietly.

For all their faults, Viv's parents tried not to argue around her, at least not like this. And they would never fight in front of Cam. If they knew they were here, they'd be embarrassed, and based on their current shouting, Cam doubted they were sober.

"Not if we're clever about it," Cam said, sliding Viv's laptop into the bag. "Come on. I got this."

Cam slowly opened the door and peeked out. Viv's parents were in the kitchen. If the girls were quick, they could slip into the living room and out the front door. Cam tried not to focus on the words Viv's parents were hurling at each other.

"I wasted the best years of my life on you!" her mother screamed.

"Oh, poor you," her father responded. "Poor, trapped Kendra. If it's such a waste, then why are you still here?"

Vivian stifled a sob. *Almost there*, Cam thought.

"Maybe I shouldn't be," Viv's mom said.

Cam's hand was on the doorknob. *Slowly, slowly.*

"Then go!" her father replied.

Cam pulled Vivian outside behind her, closing the door quietly behind them. They were free.

Viv started crying as soon as they got into the car. "I'm so embarrassed," she sobbed. "I can't believe you saw that."

Cam hugged her close. "Shhh. It's okay. It doesn't matter."

"They hate each other so much," Viv said. "You heard them. They said so. Why would two people be married who hate each other?"

"I don't know," Cam said, at a loss for words. "I don't know."

At Cam's house the girls ate cookies, and Cam painted Viv's toenails while she processed what had happened. It wasn't weird for the girls to travel between houses and sleep over at either place, so Cam's parents had only waved when they arrived.

"I just wish I had parents like yours, you know? People who actually care about each other," Viv said.

Cam didn't know what to say. "I'm so sorry, Viv. I wish I could do something to help."

"You're here," Viv said with a sad smile. "That helps."

It was early March, and RoboSub meetings were now pretty predictable. They all showed up and divided into teams. Cam was spared any weird interaction with Jeremy. Her RoboSub days were spent soldering, mapping electrical networks, and talking shop with Liam. Time flew by. It felt like one minute she put down her backpack, the next Viv tapped her on the shoulder to go. (Viv tapped carefully—she had a real fear of getting burned by a soldering iron.)

The soldering station had two seats, so Cam often found herself sitting very, very close to Liam. She learned a lot about him. He had two siblings, both younger, and he helped out a lot at home. He was nervous about leaving for college in a couple years, because his parents relied on him for babysitting in the summer and he wanted to be able to take internships. He was deep in college-search mode. He really wanted to go to Northeastern in Boston because it had work programs built in. All Cam knew about Boston was that it was a long way from Ohio.

This week when the meeting was over, Jeremy called everyone together. "Great work today, everybody. See you all next week. Cameron and Vivian, can you stay back for a minute?"

A lump formed in Cam's stomach. Viv gave her a look as they walked over to Jeremy.

"Hey. So I spoke with Mr. Lenox, and he said we need another chaperone if you two come to San Diego."

Viv and Cam just looked at him, unsure of how he wanted them to respond.

"So you can't come," he finished.

Cam felt her face heat up. Before she could respond, Vivian

waved a hand. "I'll need a moment to discuss this with my colleague," she said, and pulled Cam into the bathroom across the hall.

"Seriously, what a—" She stopped when she noticed Cam fighting back tears. "What's going on?"

"I'm just so tired of this," Cam said. She had never been the type of person to get upset at small things. She couldn't remember the last time she cried in public or even in front of anyone other than her parents or Vivian. Maybe it was the constant roadblocks Jeremy threw in her way. Maybe it was the way most CS classmates ignored her. Maybe it was all the research about the plight of women.

"I'm spending so much energy on this, you know? I'm working so hard. Why am I doing that? Am I crazy? Is it worth it?" Cam asked in exasperation.

"Whoa, whoa, whoa," Viv said, leaning against the sink. "You said this is what you want for your future. What could be more important than that? I've never known you to back down from a fight."

"I'm just so . . . afraid," Cam said. "Not of Jeremy. He's just a high school jerk. But of what he represents. He's not the only guy out there like this. He's just the first one I've come up against. I think about how bad it could get. I feel tired just thinking about it. And I'm scared it will always feel like this."

"Listen," Viv said, placing a hand on each of Cam's shoulders. "You have to be brave, like that TED Talk said. There are girls all over the world dealing with this. If they can do it, so can you."

"Jeremy will be able to tell. That I'm afraid."

"Who cares?" Viv said. "Bravery is not the absence of fear. It's feeling fear and choosing bravery anyway."

"Did you just make that up?" Cam asked.

"Nah. I think Nelson Mandela said it, or someone like that."

Cam laughed.

"Who cares what Jeremy thinks?" Viv said. "Do your thing anyway." She ripped off some paper towels and handed them to Cam. "Let's make a promise."

"Okay," Cam said, dabbing her face.

"If we're going to put ourselves in spaces that might be hostile toward us, we have to promise not to spend so much energy being upset about the circumstances. All of that could be used toward *changing* this stupid shit. Agreed?"

Cam nodded. "Agreed."

"Now, let's go back in there and rationalize this guy into oblivion. It's your superpower. I've seen you do it to your parents a million times."

Cam laughed again. "Yeah. Let's do it!"

The girls marched back into the design lab. Jeremy was packing up.

"Why exactly do we need another chaperone?" Cam asked.

Jeremy gave her a withering look. "We've got too many people for only one chaperone, so the sophomores can't come." That was them and Jackson.

"Cam and I will figure this out. We're going. Is Mr. Lenox the person we need to speak to?" Viv asked.

"I guess so."

"Great," Cam said, putting her bag on her shoulder. "You should plan on us going on the trip."

"Sure, whatever," Jeremy said, rolling his eyes. "See you later."

Cam felt triumphant. Her heart raced. Confrontation was not her thing, but she had done it and survived. They would solve this problem. They were going to San Diego.

< br >

Cam hung back at the end of the next CS class and approached Mr. Lenox while he was packing up. "Um, Mr. Lenox?"

He glanced up from his schoolbag. "Ms. Goldberg. What is it?"

"Jeremy mentioned that the sophomores on the RoboSub team might not be able to go to San Diego this summer..." she began.

"Is that what he decided? I let him know I can chaperone only ten students. I left it to his discretion to figure out who would stay behind."

It did not surprise Cam at all that Jeremy wanted to cut the sophomores. That's how he could get rid of her and Viv.

"He did, yes," Cam went on. "But it seems like we could still come. Can't we get another chaperone?"

Mr. Lenox paused. "I suppose we could. I asked in the faculty lounge, but it's difficult to convince teachers to give up part of summer to chaperone a trip."

Cam understood, but still. "If we find another chaperone, when would you need to know by?"

"We need to register by April thirtieth," he said. "So if someone agrees by mid-April, that should be okay."

One month, Cam thought. *That seems doable.* "Okay. Thank you, Mr. Lenox. We'll see what we can come up with."

"Very good," Mr. Lenox said. "And Ms. Goldberg?"

"Yeah?"

"Best to make it a female chaperone. It would be better to have one this year, if you and Ms...."

"Knix."

"Right, if you and Ms. Knix want to join us."

It's not about wanting to join. It's about having earned it, she thought.

Maybe there was more behind this than just rude Jeremy.

< br >

"Hello?" Cam called, poking her head into the sculpture studio after school the next week.

Viv had suggested her teacher, Ms. Newberry, as a potential chaperone because "she's one of the coolest ladies I've ever met." Viv had also said, "I bet she'd be down to help even in summer. Ms. Newberry is chill like that."

Soft instrumental music played, and the walls were covered in stuff. Cam expected mostly pottery: cups, plates, bowls, and vases. That's what sculpture class was, right? But a large wiry mass hung from the ceiling. It reminded Cam of the illustrations of the neurons that make up brains. There were more colors than she could count, and it was fascinating.

Along the right wall was student work in progress. While there were certainly some vases, mugs, and other kitchen sundries, there were many more projects that Cam couldn't really define in a variety of shapes and materials. Of course sculpture wasn't just clay, and Cam felt silly for making that assumption. The things in this room reminded her more of her making projects than the mugs her mom sometimes made at wine nights with her friends. Cam poked at a hexagonal object made of something solid but pliable.

A voice rang out behind her: "Come on back!"

Cam followed the sound and discovered a small room where Ms. Newberry was wrestling with what appeared to be a large piece of plastic attached to a machine.

"Um, hi. I'm Cam Goldberg."

Ms. Newberry glanced over her shoulder at Cam and smiled. "Hello, Cam Goldberg. I'm Ms. Newberry," she said. She was definitely much younger than Cam's other teachers, and more relaxed. "Could you give me a hand with this?"

"Sure," Cam said, approaching with caution. "What is it?"

"It's a vacuformer," Ms. Newberry said, pulling at the edge of the plastic. "You can use it to shape plastic into pretty much anything. Come have a look."

Trapped within the plastic was a mold of a face. "Whoa.

That's pretty cool!" Cam's mind spun with endless possibilities.

"Yeah. But it can be a real drag to get the plastic away from the mold. Helps if you pull from both sides at the same time. Grab that side, will you?"

"Oh, sure," Cam said, approaching the machine. The bottom looked like a large scale, and two pillars rose up on either side holding up what looked like a hood with a handle over the top. "How does it work?"

"Well, you place the mold on the bottom, and then you lay the thermoplastic over the top. When you push the top down, the heat melds the plastic over the mold. Once it cools, you can pull it away. Ours is a little finicky, hence the four hands instead of two."

She nodded at Cam to grab the corners. "Try to apply equal pressure all around and gently lift, if that makes sense."

"Yep. I think it does," Cam said. The supertight seal made it difficult to lift the hard plastic away, but the level of detail the machine captured was incredible.

"You could use this to make molds for quick production to make everything uniform," Cam said, thinking out loud.

"That's right," Ms. Newberry said. "That's what these machines were originally for, actually. But now a lot of 3D artists use them for fabrication."

Just then the plastic popped free. Ms. Newberry threw out a hand to grab the face as it fell. "Ha! Excellent," she said, as Cam let go. "Thanks for the help."

"No problem," Cam said. "So, Vivian Knix is a good friend of mine—"

"Ah, Ms. Knix!" Ms. Newberry said, leading Cam back out into the main studio. "An excellent student and quick to learn new things."

Cam nodded. "We're on the RoboSub team together, and we need another chaperone to come to San Diego in July. We were hoping that you might consider coming on the trip with us."

Ms. Newberry sat down on a stool and wiped her hands with a towel. "The Robo what?"

"RoboSub. It's a competition where teams make autonomous underwater vehicles and compete at a live competition every year at the TRANSDEC in San Diego."

"The what?"

"It's short for Transducer Evaluation Center."

"Right," Ms. Newberry said with a grin.

"Anyway, there are a lot of team members, so we need a second chaperone. And Viv and I are the only girls on the team. The faculty advisor said he'd prefer if the second chaperone was a woman."

"And he sent you to find one?" She looked doubtful.

"Well, no. He told the club president to decide how to handle it. So Jeremy decided we just shouldn't go. But Viv and I don't accept that."

Ms. Newberry let out a guffaw. "That sounds like Ms. Knix." Her face grew concerned. "I haven't heard about this. Why hasn't the advisor reached out to faculty to find another chaperone?" she asked. "Who's the advisor?"

"Mr. Lenox," Cam said.

Ms. Newberry made a face, opened her mouth, closed it, and took a breath. "I see. And now you and Ms. Knix can't go to this robot boat competition—"

"RoboSub."

"Right, RoboSub. Well, how about you send me the dates, and I'll see what I can do?"

"Really? That would be so, so great," Cam said, amazed it had been so easy.

Ms. Newberry shrugged. "Why not? If you're anything like Ms. Knix, then I'm sure the two of you are working hard for that team and deserve to go. If I can help, I'll be happy to."

"Thank you so much, Ms. Newberry. We really appreciate it."

"No problem," she said. As Cam started to leave Ms. Newberry added, "Ms. Goldberg, why haven't I seen you in this studio before?"

"Oh, I'm taking the computer science elective," Cam said.

"An excellent excuse," Ms. Newberry teased with a warm smile. "And are you enjoying it?"

Cam shrugged. "I like to make things, but honestly I thought it would be different."

Ms. Newberry studied Cam's face. "You know, if you'd ever like to come explore the tools in this studio, please feel welcome," she said. "I'm generally available, and you might be surprised by how much overlap there is between what I do and what Mr. Lenox is up to in the design lab."

Cam smiled. "Thanks, I definitely will," she said. And she meant it.

"Oh, and Cam?"

"Yeah?"

"What you said about a female chaperone for the trip— that's not a thing. I take students to the MCA in Chicago every year. I've never needed a male chaperone for male students."

```
(function imposter(){
    console.log("Chapter");
    console.log("Eleven");
})();
```

Chapter Eleven

As March dragged on, Cam fell into a routine. RoboSub meetings became pretty normal, and Cam enjoyed working with the soldering irons and other tools in the design lab. Liam went out of his way to show her how to use everything, and he was always willing to talk her through parts of the sub so she could catch up. She tried not to read into that. Besides, Viv read into it enough for both of them.

Cam and Jackson's game was taking shape, and it was time to prototype gameplay items. Ms. Newberry and the vacuformer had piqued Cam's interest. She built a utility belt (complete with a small air horn to disarm Blockheads and scrunchies to pull back hair for battle) in the sculpture studio and started on different weapons.

Vivian was often in the studio after school. The written part of her project for the ICDC was due the first week of April, and Cam suspected Viv wanted to avoid home. The girls hadn't discussed what happened with Viv's parents any further. Sometimes Viv would gaze off, distracted and sad. Cam knew better than to push. Viv would bring it up in her own time.

Viv kept badgering Cam about guys, probably as a distraction. "That Liam fellow is pretty nice," she said, flipping through glaze samples.

"Fellow? Yep. He's a good team leader. Treats everyone fairly, and patient with teaching new things."

"Mmm," Viv said. "And sort of cute."

"I guess so," Cam replied. Being around Liam made her stomach hurt, and she didn't like it.

"I heard he broke up with his girlfriend in the fall."

"Maybe you should ask him to hang out sometime," Cam said.

"I told you!" Viv said with a huff, "I decided to wait for college. No one at MacArthur can meet my needs."

"And I told *you*," Cam replied, "that I am too." But she thought, *Liam does smell nice* . . .

"Oh, fine. Fair enough," Viv retorted. "Hey, let's see what Jackson's up to."

Cam shrugged at her and went back to work. Viv logged in to Battle.net and chatted with Jackson regularly. They hadn't exchanged real names, which seemed typical in the gaming world. That meant that Viv knew who she was talking to, but Jackson had no idea. Cam had almost casually mentioned it one day, but Vivian kicked her hard under the table.

"Ha! Ohmigod!" Viv said, putting a hand over her mouth.

Cam shot her an annoyed look.

"Sorry. Jackson just said something really funny."

"You know, if you and Jackson are getting along so well, maybe you should hang out with him in person sometime."

"You know he's not my type."

"Do I?" Cam asked. "You haven't dated anyone since Teddy in the eighth grade."

"And I will respectfully remind you that we do not speak of that!" Viv snapped.

"Right, that which we do not speak of. I just don't really know your type. I mean, I know your celebrity type, of course."

Viv nodded. "Jordan face, Glover personality, Elba body."

"Right," Cam said. "But I'm not sure how that translates into, you know . . . a real person."

"Such a person does not exist," Viv replied. "I am destined to waste the prime of my youth pining for a partner who simply will not arrive."

"Please. That's a little much."

"It's just the truth," Viv said, turning back to her laptop and giggling again.

"Will you ever tell Jackson that PrezRoslin is you?" Cam asked.

"God, no."

Cam wondered what Viv feared more: that things might be awkward in real life or that Jackson would stop talking to her online. They'd been messaging on Battle.net for over a month. That was a long time. Jackson thought he was talking to a random girl. The deception made Cam uncomfortable.

"What do you think?" Cam said, holding up the figurine she'd just finished. It was a model of a Blockhead complete with cube-shaped head, extra-large hands, and a perpetually scowling face. And a business suit, of course.

"I love it," Viv said, leaning in to take a closer look. "I love his little unibrow."

"You don't think it's too much?" Cam asked.

"You mean the unibrow?"

"No. I just don't wanna be mean, you know? Like, in our mission to empower women, I don't think we should put down men."

"Very noble of you," Viv said. "I don't think it's too much. Parts of the female character are exaggerated too. It's part of the art."

"Cool," Cam said, packing up her stuff.

"Ladies! Good afternoon," Ms. Newberry said, stopping at their table. "I checked the dates, and I'm happy to join you in San Diego."

"Yass!" Viv cried.

Cam laughed. "Thank you so much, Ms. Newberry. We'll let Mr. Lenox know."

"I'd like to handle that, actually," Ms. Newberry said, a shadow passing over her face. "Don't worry about a thing."

That weekend Cam was roped into going to her mom's office to help clean out some filing cabinets and organize. "I'll pay you!" Mom had promised. "Please, I'm so behind."

They had a new office assistant, Marissa, who needed training, and Cam's mom was the only one willing to spend the time. Cam caught her mom up about the field trip and Ms. Newberry while they worked. Marissa was updating online listings.

"I cannot believe that Mr. Lenox. He's letting that boy Jeremy do whatever he pleases. I want to call the school," Mom said.

"I know, but I'm glad you haven't," Cam said. "It would only make it worse. Guys like Jeremy don't respond well to being told what to do."

"Ugh. Yes," Marissa said. "I'm familiar with the type."

As if on cue, they heard the *beep-beep* of someone locking a car out front, and Shane entered the office.

"I'm tellin' you, there's no time for an inspection! I've got four other offers, and we're ready to walk! It's up to you, but it'll be your deal to lose," Shane shouted into his phone. His arms were full of folders and papers. He nodded at Cam's mom when he saw them. "I'm hangin' up, Jerry—take it or leave it!" he said, sliding the phone into his pocket. "I don't actually have any other offers. That guy's a bozo. Am I right?" he said, glancing at Marissa.

She gave a little laugh.

"Ladies, burning the midday oil. How's it goin'?" he asked, dropping all the papers at the largest desk in the middle of the room.

"Hi, Mr. Brooks," Marissa said. She was clearly trying to impress her new boss.

"Hi, Shane," Cam's mom said. "Doing well. How are you?"

Mom was being polite, but Shane leapt at the chance to keep talking. Cam cringed.

"I got this nuts-for-brains buyer's agent trying to get an inspection on Harris Street, and I'm like, we're not waiting three weeks for that to happen. What do you think this is, Arkansas? I can move that property by next week." He scooped a handful of M&M'S from the corner of his desk and kept talking while he chewed. "Besides, the owner told me they've got a little radon problem they never mitigated. If there's no inspection, we don't gotta disclose that." He grinned a little creepily at Cam. "Little trick for ya: if they inspect and find something, the seller usually drops the price—and our commission."

"Cam's here to help me finish up a few things," Cam's mom said, saving Cam from having to respond. "And Marissa is updating the online listings."

"Brilliant! And how is our newest team member doing?" Shane asked, sauntering over to Marissa's desk. She showed him her work and asked a few questions.

"Ohmigod. Thank you so much. You are the kindest, most beautiful mother," Cam whisper-gushed.

Mom laughed. "Just keep your head down. He'll get bored and leave soon."

"Help me find those new coffee cups we ordered, will ya?" Shane said too loudly.

Marissa followed him to the back where the kitchen was.

Cam was sorting through old pamphlets when she heard a clatter and yelp from the kitchen. Shane rushed out, grabbed something off his desk, and flew out the main door without even saying goodbye.

"What was that?" Cam's mom asked, her brow furrowing. "Marissa? Everything okay?"

No response. Mom stood up, and Marissa appeared in the kitchen doorway. Her arms were crossed, and tears stained her cheeks.

"Marissa?" Cam's mother took a step toward her. "Are you okay?"

"I didn't... I don't." Marissa burst into tears. Mom rushed to hug her, and Cam stood up.

"Are you hurt? Come sit down," Mom said, leading Marissa to her desk. "What's going on? What happened?" Mom asked.

"I... I was just..." Marissa began, still crying. "He grabbed me."

Cam's mother's face got dark, unlike anything Cam had seen before. "What do you mean?"

"It was..." Marissa paused again.

"It's okay. You're in shock. Tell us in your own time."

Marissa glanced at Cam, then leaned in to Mom and whispered. "He grabbed my... my backside."

Mom made her *tch* sound and took in a sharp breath. "Ay, ese man es un morón."

"I was showing him where the new coffee stuff is, and he came up behind me—"

"You did nothing wrong," Cam's mom said, putting her arms around Marissa. "That man is repulsive."

Cam didn't know what to do. The women seemed to forget about her. She was lost in her thoughts. *Did Shane really do that with us sitting in the next room? What the fuck?*

Marissa suddenly perked up. "Oh my god. What do I do now? Do . . . do you think he'll fire me?"

"Oh, Marissa—" Cam's mother began.

"I really need this job. When he . . . When it happened, I dropped a coffee mug because I was so surprised. He just ran out. What if he thinks I'm going to report him?"

"You *should* report it!" Cam said.

Her mom's face flashed different emotions: anger to surprise to concern. Neither woman responded at first.

"You're going to report it, right?" Cam asked. "Mom, you could say something."

Cam's mom looked at Marissa, who blew her nose. "These things can be tricky," Mom said. "People don't always believe what you tell them."

"But we're here," Cam said. "We heard what happened."

Cam's mother's expression was pained. She exchanged a glance with Marissa. "It's definitely up to you. I'll do whatever you choose."

Marissa nodded, sniffling. Cam was incredulous. She opened her mouth to protest, but her mother shot her a look that made it clear she shouldn't keep pressing.

Not now, Mom mouthed.

Cam exploded when they got in the car about twenty minutes later. "Mom, we have to say something! Are you really thinking about not saying anything?"

Mom sighed as she turned on the car. "It's not so simple, nena. These things can get very sticky."

"Sticky how?"

"Who would we tell? Shane is in charge of our office, so we'd have to go to the owner. Who's to say if he would do anything about it?"

"Well he *has* to, doesn't he?"

Her mother's frustration was clear. "Says who?"

Cam thought it through. If her mom reported the incident, and the owner didn't do anything, the next step would be . . . the police?

"The police, right? Or Marissa could get a lawyer?"

Her mother shook her head. "Lawyers are expensive. And what if they fire her? How will she make money to pay the lawyer?"

Dread filled Cam. The whole situation was appalling. Marissa was doing her work. How could it be okay that some guy—a guy in charge—could just breeze in and do whatever he wanted with no consequences?

At the same time, what her mom was saying made sense. It could be even worse. Marissa didn't deserve any of this.

"Well, what the fuck!" Cam said.

Mom did a double take. Cam rarely swore in front of her parents.

"What's anyone supposed to do about things like this?"

They pulled into their driveway. Mom put the car in park and turned to Cam. "Cam, I agree with you. I want you to know that. And if Marissa wants me to say something, I definitely will. I want you to know that too. But this woman's livelihood is at stake, and we just have to be careful. I'm sorry you had to see it. I'm . . ." She looked out the window at a loss for words. "I'm sorry this happens at all." She paused, then slammed both hands against the wheel. "¡Puta madre!"

< br >

Cam and her mom were quiet at dinner. Dad kept looking between them, but Mom just waved her hand as if to say *Later*.

Cam kept thinking about how Marissa looked when she appeared in the doorway: so shocked and upset. How Shane had just breezed out and gone on with his day. And now Marissa had to worry about losing her job, even if she didn't report him. The unfairness gave Cam a migraine.

"I'm going to bed," she said.

"You haven't touched your food," Dad pointed out. "Is everything okay?"

Mom reached out and put a hand on his arm. "It's okay, nena. Let us know if you need anything, okay?"

"Sure, whatever," Cam said and fled to her room.

Conflicting feelings raced through her. Frustration that her mom wasn't doing more. Understanding about why she wasn't. Anger at the whole situation. And of course, the connection to everything she'd read about in the tech industry. *Is this the kind of bullshit women are dealing with?* she thought. No wonder they were staging walkouts and quitting. Why bother putting up with this kind of thing?

But Cam also felt in her gut that quitting wasn't an answer. Sure, if Marissa got a different job, she wouldn't have to see Shane anymore. But who's to say there wasn't a Shane at her next job? Or the one after that? When did it stop?

Did it ever stop?

```
(function imposter(){
    console.log("Chapter");
    console.log("Twelve");
})();
```

Chapter Twelve

Cam still had no appetite the next morning. Dad offered her coffee and a bagel, but he was moving with extreme caution. Clearly Mom had filled him in.

Cam moved through her classes like a zombie, not really hearing her teachers, just going through the motions. Even Viv was at a loss for words when she heard the story. "That is so fucked," she said.

At RoboSub, Cam stayed late so she could finish some connections on the sub. Spring break was coming up, and the design lab would be closed the whole time. Cam and Jackson also needed to turn in their project, so she was trying to get ahead with RoboSub before she got too busy with other school stuff. Viv had to go to a DECA meeting and was around less and less as the ICDC grew closer.

Several others had stayed late too, although they didn't seem to be getting much work done. Cam moved so she could focus, rolling the soldering cart over to an empty workbench. Working quietly on her own was calming—she tried to block out everything and focus on the work. Still, conversation drifted over to her from the laser cutter.

"This stuff from Vivian is great," Liam said. Cam felt her stomach flutter a little at the compliment for her friend. It was nice of Liam to notice.

"Yeah, she really crushed the sponsorship asks," Matt added.

A small smile formed on Cam's lips.

"Whatever. We could've gotten this stuff," Jeremy countered.

"What do you mean?" Matt asked.

"We could've gotten it without her. It was just easier for her because people don't want to say no to a girl."

The boys laughed, and Cam bristled.

"I heard she wouldn't leave the NTL office until they agreed to pay for new thrusters," Spencer said.

More laughter from the group, over the word *thrusters*, Cam guessed. *So immature*, she thought.

"Her persistence is kind of cool, though," Matt said.

Dan, a senior, chimed in. "I sent my sister to GameStop to pick up the new *Fortnite*, and they gave her a 20 percent discount for literally no reason. Like they'd never seen a girl in there before and were willing to give her whatever."

"Dude, really? I gotta get my sister to go for me!" Matt said.

"Totally. And Vivian'd probably get an even bigger discount," Dan said.

Cam's ears were getting hot.

"Did you see what she wore to the basketball game last week?" Jeremy asked.

The laughter got louder. Cam couldn't stop herself from looking. Liam wasn't laughing.

"Some girls are just asking for it," Jeremy added.

The electrical connection Cam was working on overheated. "Excuse me?" she asked.

The laughter stopped completely, and all the boys turned to Cam. They looked surprised, like they'd forgotten she was there. No one responded.

"What did you just say?" Cam asked, putting the soldering iron aside and standing up.

Jeremy's face was blank. Cam knew he had a choice: back down in front of his friends or double down and make it a show. She knew which one he'd pick.

"You heard me," he said. "Some girls dress a certain way to get attention. Everybody knows that."

Take a deep breath, Cam thought.

And then she saw the smug look on his face—like Shane—and enough was enough. "Do you even understand what you're saying?" she asked, her face on fire.

He just looked at her.

Obviously he knew what he'd said, but that wasn't Cam's problem. After all her time reading accounts from women in tech, hearing about Jackson's sister, and then seeing what happened to Marissa, Cam was done. This bullshit was all connected.

Maybe her mother was too afraid to speak up. Not Cam. Not anymore.

"I'll break it down for you. First, you're implying that girls make decisions to attract attention from guys. Like we couldn't possibly have a different reason to care how we look. Like, say, I don't know, our own self-esteem, maybe."

Cam saw Matt smile. She took a deep breath to calm her nerves.

"Second, you assume that we're trying to attract *your* attention." She waved at the broader group. "Any of your attention. Do you realize how entitled that is? Like, you're so incredible that we need to set some kind of trap with our clothes and makeup just to get you to... what? Talk to us? Well, let me be clear—you're not on our wish list."

A few boys laughed a little and then stifled it when Jeremy shot them a look.

Cam continued, "Or do you mean the third thing: that girls dress a certain way to signal to you, Jeremy, king of men, that they want you to touch them?"

He actually blushed, which made Cam feel bolder. She took a step closer.

"Do you think they want to date you, Jeremy? Do you think that's why girls wear a nice dress or a new pair of jeans?"

Another step forward. He looked down.

"Do you think they want you to grab them? Would that be fine if their outfit said 'I'm asking for it'? Do you think you're entitled to my body, because you're so amazing and I'm just a girl?"

"Jesus, Cam. I was just kidding."

She was right in front of him now. Her voice was firm, loud. "No. You. Weren't. And that's what creates a culture where girls aren't safe. That's what creates a culture where I can't go somewhere without texting my parents when I arrive."

Jeremy shifted like he was going to interrupt her, but Matt put out a hand to stop him.

So she went on. "That's what creates a culture where a Supreme Court nominee can sexually assault a woman, that woman can testify to Congress that it happened, and we *still* put that guy on the court. And you know what guys like that say? Guys like you? They say we're asking for it by how we dress or what we drink or the way we breathe. So you know what?"

She took a step back, looking at them all. "Let me give all of you a piece of advice. We're not asking for it. Ever. Not your attention. Not your words. Not your gross hands. Just leave us the hell alone."

At that point she wanted to storm out. But she hadn't unplugged the soldering iron, and she really didn't want to accidentally break equipment. So she stomped over to her worktable, unplugged everything, grabbed her bag, and *then* stormed out.

As she passed through the doorway, she ran into Viv.

"Oh, hey!" Viv said. "Sorry I'm running so late, I—"

"Let's go." Cam grabbed Viv's arm and pulled her down the hall into an empty classroom. Then she burst into tears.

"Cam, what happened! What's going on?" Viv asked.

Through her blubbering, Cam told Viv the whole story. Viv listened without interruption (other than mumbling *asshole* a time or two). Then she hugged Cam tight.

"Girl, that is amazing. I love you so much. Thank you for saying those things. And you're right." She leaned back to look at Cam. "Everything you said was totally right."

"I know, but that's even worse," Cam said, fresh tears falling. "I don't *want* to be right. I don't want to live in a world like this. We have a one-in-three chance of experiencing sexual violence in our lives. One in three, Viv! I don't want that to happen to me. I don't want to be afraid all the time."

Vivian hugged her again. "I know. Me neither."

"I feel powerless, you know? Like, this has been going on for so long, and what are people doing about it? What is my *mom* doing about it? And how can we make it different? Stupid guys like Jeremy are never going to change. They think the world revolves around them. How can we keep him from harming someone someday? You know it's going to happen. Him—and guys like him—they grow up and they grab girls at parties or put things in their drinks. Our parents always warn us, but why is it our responsibility? Why aren't parents telling their *sons* to act differently, instead of telling *us* to be on guard?"

Vivian shook her head. "I don't know, Cam. When you put it like that, it sounds pretty ridiculous."

Cam placed her hands over her eyes and pushed a little bit, the pressure calming her down. "I'm so tired of this, and it's only been three months," she said. "I'm gonna encounter guys like Jeremy my entire life."

Viv put a hand on hers. "Yeah, you're probably right. But think about it this way: What do those guys want?"

"What do they want?"

"Yeah. What is their goal?"

Cam thought about it. For Jeremy the answer was clear. "They want me to quit. To leave the program so they can have it to themselves."

"Exactly," Viv said. "Oprah once said that success is the best revenge. You want to show those guys what a girl can do? Then show them. But whatever you do, do not let them win. Don't let them drive you away, because if you do that, they win. And worse, they learn that the strategy works, and they'll do it again and again. So you know what I think? I think you stay."

"How do I do that?" Cam asked.

"With help from friends," Viv said, squeezing her hand. "And a lot of ice cream. I feel like TV ads want me to think that baths help, but I haven't tested that one."

Cam laughed through her tears and wiped her face. "Thanks, Viv. I love you."

"I love you too, Cam."

< br >

When Cam got home, she beelined past her parents and up to her room. She was in no mood to tell anyone about her day. About thirty minutes later there was a soft knock on her door.

"Cam?" It was Dad.

"Yeah. Come in," she said. She had already changed into

her favorite pajamas and her bunny slippers, which she'd had since middle school. She was lying on her bed, clutching a pillow and staring at the ceiling.

"Hey, hon," he said, closing the door behind him. "Everything okay?"

Cam just shrugged.

"Hard day at school?"

Cam sighed. He wasn't going to leave until she spilled some information. "I kind of exploded at this jerk Jeremy from Robo-Sub today."

He sat on the foot of her bed. "Oh yeah? Tell me more."

This wasn't really something she wanted to discuss with her father. She wasn't nervous about talking to her dad about her life. She always had. It was more that she didn't want to reveal how hard it was to be a girl in the spaces she'd recently put herself. Or to be a girl at all, really. He always tried to be empathetic, but it just wasn't possible for him to know what it was like. What she really needed was Mom. *But she might say I caused more trouble than it's worth*, she thought. That brought tears to her eyes. She clutched the pillow a little tighter and shrugged again.

"I really wanna help," he said, still trying.

"I guess . . ." Cam started, her voice uneven. "I guess I'm frustrated. And disappointed. About the guys at school. About all guys." She allowed herself a calming pause, then went on. "And I'm doing all this research about how women are treated, and it's really a bummer. And I'm also, like, already dealing with this stuff. It feels like there's nothing I can do about it. I blew up at these guys, and who even knows if it'll make a difference."

Her father took a deep breath, then nodded and put a hand on the bunny-slippered foot closest to him. "That's a tough one, Cam."

She wiped her face and sat up a little. "I know."

They sat in silence for a moment. "I wish I had an easy answer," he said. "But I just don't. This is one of those things I can't fix for you, as much as I'd like to. It's bigger than us." He straightened up, turning to face her more fully. "I hate seeing stuff like this, whether at your school, my work, or the grocery store. I can't make it stop, but I can promise that when I see something, I'll say something. Do you believe me?"

She looked in his eyes and saw he meant it, so she nodded.

"And I usually find there are more good guys than there are Jeremys. They just don't always know how to show it."

"Guys have less to lose," she said.

"Yes and no. Bullying by guys like Jeremy goes in all directions. It's just different for guys. I've felt pressure to go along with it in my life. I thought if I didn't, I wasn't cool, or I might get picked on, or I might get fired. It's just different."

She hadn't considered that before. "We have to stop letting a handful of people cause all this social garbage. It's such a colossal waste of energy."

He wrapped his arms around her. "You're right. You're totally right."

He left her room, and she heard him and her mom in the hallway.

"Is she okay?" Mom asked.

"No," Dad replied. "But I think she will be."

```
(function imposter(){
    console.log("Chapter");
    console.log("Thirteen");
})();
```

Chapter Thirteen

A few days later, Cam was at Aldo's with Jackson and Viv again. Viv was on her laptop, closing a few deals with local businesses to get parts for the RoboSub. Jackson was, as usual, gaming.

"We really need to work on our video component after spring break," Viv said.

"Oh yeah. What's the theme again?" Cam asked.

"Sixties," Viv said.

"So what's that? Like, big hair and pastel appliances?" Jackson said.

Even though he was gaming, Jackson was usually listening to the conversations around him. It wasn't clear to Cam how or when he did his homework, but he did everything on time for their project, and he did a good job.

Cam googled "the sixties" and scanned the results. "Looks like it was the decade of peace, love, and rock 'n' roll."

"Hmmm," Viv said. "How important is the video to our overall score?"

"Not that much, actually," Cam said, skimming through the RoboSub scoring rubric.

"Great. I doubt we're gonna get Oscar-worthy acting out of those guys," Jackson said. They all laughed.

"Damn!" he said, pushing his laptop away. From what Cam could tell, he didn't lose often. When he did, he usually had a brief outburst, got a snack, and went back to playing.

"What map were you on?" Viv said, without looking up from her laptop.

"Blackheart's Bay," he replied, then did a double take. "Wait. What?"

"Hmm?" Viv said, looking up from her laptop.

Cam froze. Viv wasn't supposed to know anything about *Heroes of the Storm*.

Viv realized what she'd done and tried to recover. "Oh, um, I just noticed that when you play that thingy, the board is sometimes different, so I figured there are different locations and stuff."

He looked at her, clearly skeptical.

"Whatever. Just trying to make conversation. Don't have to make it awkward!" she said.

Viv didn't often get flustered. Cam tried to hide a grin.

"Anyway," Viv said, "does anybody want breadsticks? I could do breadsticks. I'm gonna go get some."

"She can be pretty weird sometimes," Jackson said as Viv walked away.

"Yep," Cam said. *You have no idea*.

< br >

That evening, Cam's dad was out late for a work meeting, and Cam was home alone with her mom. Over the past few days,

Cam kept wondering, *What's happening with Marissa?* but she felt like she shouldn't ask. And her mom didn't bring it up. Cam was so disappointed—especially in her mom.

When Cam came down from her room to scrounge together some dinner, she was surprised to find that Mom had made Tuscan mac and cheese—Cam's favorite.

"Oh, nena. I wanted to surprise you. Surprise!"

"Oh, um. Thanks," Cam said, taking a seat at the table. She picked at the food in silence for a few minutes until Mom started talking.

"Nena, I know you have not been very happy with me lately."

Cam shrugged.

Her mother sighed. "Honestly, I'm not very happy with myself."

That piqued Cam's interest.

"I've been thinking a lot about what I told you, after what happened with Marissa. About there not really being anything she—or we—could do."

Cam nodded.

"Well, that's bullshit."

Cam almost dropped her fork.

"I see what you put up with at school—and I know you're pushing back. Your dad told me. I know I encouraged you not to start trouble and to keep your head down." She took a deep breath. "That advice is crap. I'm sorry."

"Really?"

"Yeah, really," Mom said. "What happened with Marissa got me thinking. I've worked at that firm for twelve years, and when they needed a new manager, it should've been me. When they hired Shane, I didn't say a thing. I told myself there must be a reason. Maybe he's more qualified or a better salesperson. All bullshit, clearly."

Very clearly, Cam thought. *Shane is an asshole.*

"And if I'd pushed back, if I'd done something—I don't even know what, demanded more answers, or demanded the job—this wouldn't have happened to Marissa at all. And now what am I doing? Staying silent?" Mom shook her head. "She deserves better. I deserve better. We all do. And no one's gonna hand anything to women if we keep our heads down."

Cam's chest swelled with hope.

Mom took a sip of her wine. "I chatted with the other agents at work—you know, Cecilia, Barry, and Ramon? They're tired of Shane too. We're going to make a complaint to the owner together. We'll be stronger together."

"What about Marissa?"

Her mom thought for a few seconds. "I still think it's her story to tell. I wouldn't share the details without her permission. But if we feel confident we can remove him anyway, or that sharing won't affect her job, then I will. And I hope they fire that fucker."

"Mom!" Cam laughed. Usually Mom swore only in Spanish.

Her mom laughed back. "I mean it! I hope they do!" She leaned over and put a hand on Cam's. "You inspire me, nena. You inspire me to do more. To be the change, not just dream about it. And I'm going to do it now."

< br >

The next morning Cam peered into her locker, trying to recall which books she needed before lunch, when she sensed someone on the other side of the door. Poking her head out, she found Matt.

"Hey," he said. He looked nervous.

"Hi," Cam responded, closing the door a little.

"I just wanted to say that I'm sorry about Jeremy the other day," he said.

Cam looked at him.

"Well, no, I mean . . ." Matt sighed. "He shouldn't have said those things, and I'm sorry that I didn't say anything. When he made those comments about Vivian."

Cam raised an eyebrow.

"Obviously I've heard him say stuff like that before—guys say stuff like that all the time. And I always figure they're just trying to show off or be macho or whatever, or that it's just the way guys talk, you know?"

"No," Cam said. "I don't."

"Right, of course not," Matt said, looking flustered. "So you said that thing about women getting assaulted. I looked that up the other night, and I found all this stuff about misogyny and rape culture and violence against women. My sister's in college—did you know that?"

Cam shook her head.

"She told me once that she walks at night with her car keys poking out through her fingers in case anyone tries to attack her. When she told me, I was like, *What the hell; that's so weird.* But then I read all this stuff and . . . it's all part of the same thing. And that's what you were saying, right?"

Cam stared at him and thought, *Did I really get through to him?* "Yeah. Pretty much."

He let out a huff of air and ran a hand through his hair. "It's fucked up. You're right. And Jeremy can be a real dick sometimes."

Cam laughed.

"Last year he made comments about my mom making us sandwiches and stuff all the time. Like dude, fuck off." He looked off to the distance. "She'd actually kill me if she knew I allowed Jeremy to say that stuff," he mumbled, almost to himself. "Anyway. I'm sorry. I can't undo anything. But I can stand up to Jeremy from now on. He listens to me, because we go way back."

There was a pause, like he was waiting for Cam to accept his apology.

This is not enough, she thought. "Look," she said, grabbing the last book she needed and closing her locker. "I'm glad you realized all that stuff, but you're one guy. One guy out of, like, millions of guys. We can't make change with just you."

He looked crestfallen, which made her feel a little bad for him. She remembered what her dad said, about how bullies can turn on guys too. How it can be hard to stand up to them.

"I'm not saying it doesn't help. But when you say you'll speak up, I need you to mean it. And more than just to Jeremy. I need you to say something to anybody, everybody, when you hear stupid garbage. I need you to explain why their behavior is so dangerous, and why it needs to stop. When you do that, many guys aren't going to want to hear it, and *that's* when it's actually the most important."

Matt nodded. "I hear that. I do mean it. Can I be, like . . . an ally?"

"No." Cam scoffed. "Women don't need allies. We need accomplices."

"I'm going to do more," he said. "And I'm sorry I haven't done more before now."

"Thank you. You should know that Viv and I had to find the second chaperone for San Diego or Jeremy was going to leave us behind."

Matt looked surprised. "I didn't know that. I totally support you coming. And I'm sorry you had to find the chaperone. I'll make sure Jeremy knows you're both definitely coming."

Vivian passed Matt as he was walking away, saw his face, and came over to Cam. "What happened?"

"He apologized for not doing more to stop Jeremy from being such a jerk," Cam replied.

"Wow," Viv said, glancing back at Matt. "That's pretty cool."

"Yeah," Cam said. "It's a good start."

That night Cam dreamed she was in the video game she and Jackson were creating.

She blasted Blockheads with her Ring of Power. Vaulting over desks and kicking down closed doors, she ran, rolled, and somersaulted through the office building until she came to the Boss—it was Jeremy.

She was doing significant damage, but then he called down a horde of tiny Blockheads that swarmed all around her. There were too many of them.

She pushed a button on her phone and called for backup. Three figures appeared. On Cam's right: Vivian, looking like Captain Marvel with sick aviators and a bomber jacket over her business jumpsuit. On Cam's left: Mom, with nails like Catwoman that she bared like a leopard. And behind Cam . . . Matt? He was dressed in ripped business pants and a button-down with the sleeves torn off. He winked and held out his arm. A bright-purple beam shot out of his watch and expanded in front of them. The Blockheads scattered.

With the Blockheads out of the way, Cam had a clear shot at Jeremy. Charging, she leapt in the air and brought down a crippling blow with her sensible heel. He exploded into sparkly confetti that also destroyed the Blockheads.

Cam and her helpers cheered. But an evil laugh interrupted them. Everything went dark. A word flashed, like in old arcade games. A single word, a simple question: Continue?

Cam snapped awake, breathing fast. *Holy shit*, she thought.

Her problem wouldn't go away with Jeremy. He was a symptom, not the cause. He was just one bad guy—the boss at the end of the first level—and Cam still had a whole game to play.

The next day in class, Mr. Lenox came in and started writing on the board. Cam heard whispering from the back of the room, as usual, but she ignored it and took notes. About ten minutes later, Cam heard Matt.

"I mean it, that's enough!" he said.

Cam spun around to see Jeremy looking shocked.

"It's not funny," Matt added as he gathered up his notebook and his laptop. He took his bag and moved to the middle of the room, between the boys and Cam. "Sorry, Mr. Lenox."

Mr. Lenox looked puzzled but didn't dwell on it. He turned back to the board and resumed writing. Cam looked at Matt over her shoulder. He made eye contact and nodded. The image of him from her dream flashed through her mind.

Thank you, she mouthed, smiled, and got back to work in peace.

Later Cam met up with Viv for lunch.

"Ugh, I am so ready for spring break," Viv said.

Only two more classes before two blissful weeks off. Cam planned to finish the proposal for her Girls Who Code chapter. She knew exactly who she wanted to be the advisor.

"Are you sure Ms. Newberry doesn't already advise a club?" she asked Viv.

"Yep," Viv said. "Someone in her advisory told me."

Cam was now really comfortable working in the studio. Something about how Ms. Newberry set it up made everything accessible. There were clear signs with directions about how to use everything, and even Ms. Newberry's attitude made it a safe, easy place to hang out and explore making. It was exactly the kind of vibe Cam wanted for her new club.

"Are you at all excited about Aruba?" she asked Viv.

Viv's parents had booked a trip—seven days in Aruba at a

resort condo. Viv had expected the "we're getting a divorce" talk when her parents sat her down and made the trip announcement.

"Ugh. You mean our Swiss Family Robinson act?" Viv said. "It's bad enough in our own house with our own rooms and cars and the freedom to leave whenever we need a break. Stranding ourselves in a two-bedroom apartment on an island is a literal nightmare."

"We can FaceTime every night," Cam reminded her.

"In theory," she replied. "We'll see what the service is like. I already told Jackson I might be offline for a couple weeks, just in case," she added, sipping from her soda.

"What?" Cam asked, eyebrows raised.

"You know, since we play *HotS*, like, every night," Viv replied.

"Did you just say *HotS*?"

"You know, *Heroes of the Storm*."

"I know what *HotS* stands for. I'm just surprised *you* know."

Viv shrugged. "I've been playing pretty regularly."

"Like, playing in general, or playing with Jackson?"

"Playing with Jackson," Viv said, trying to sound nonchalant.

Cam flashed her a look.

"What! It's a fun game. I'm learning a lot about it!"

"Then play with randos!"

"Gross. Too many people on there are rude to me."

Cam shook her head.

"What?"

"You're probably spending more time with him than I am," Cam said.

"It's no big deal," Viv said. "Just friendly gaming."

"Have you told him who you are?"

"Lord, no," Viv said.

"Viv, are you serious?"

"What? It doesn't come up! It's not cool to push for personal details. And besides, it would be weird if I was like, 'Oh, by the way, I'm Viv, and I've known who you are this whole time and never said anything.'"

"That's exactly what you should do!" Cam said.

Viv shushed her. "Keep your voice down! You're drawing attention."

"Viv, Jackson is my friend. I feel weird about this secret."

"Do his gaming habits come up often?"

"No," Cam said.

"Well, then, it's not a lie. You're just . . . neglecting to mention it. It's an act of omission."

"He's going to find out eventually," Cam said.

"Naaah," Viv replied. "Remember when we catfished Nathan in seventh grade? With that fake Instagram account when we pretended to be my boyfriend from another school? That guy *still* doesn't know that was us."

"I'm not particularly proud of that," Cam said, blushing at the memory.

Nathan had a crush on Viv, and when he told her in gym class, she panicked and said she had a boyfriend. That started a rumor that her boyfriend went to another school. So Cam and Viv made a fake Instagram account and messaged a few people to verify his existence. It all worked easily, and when they got bored, they wrote fake breakup posts. Viv acted heartbroken for a few days. It got her a lot of attention, especially since most people weren't dating at all then. To this day people still treated her like she had some mystical access to boys outside of school. But this situation felt different.

"Look. *If* it somehow comes up, I promise to be honest with him," Viv said.

"You mean that?" Cam asked.

Viv stuck out her pinkie finger. "Pinkie promise." The two

girls swore on it. "Now, let's go see if Ms. Newberry is around."

When they arrived in the studio, Ms. Newberry was wrestling with what appeared to be a giant sculpture of a dinosaur head.

"Ms. Knix, Ms. Goldberg. Always a pleasure," she said. "Would you mind handing me those pliers?"

Viv went over to grab them. "What's this?" she asked.

"An advanced studio project," she said. "One of my students is creating a life-size animatronic T. rex."

"Like in *Jurassic Park*?" Cam asked.

"Yes, exactly!"

"Cool," Viv said. She glanced at Cam and motioned for her to get the conversation going.

"Um, Ms. Newberry, we were hoping we could ask you about something. Is this an okay time?"

"Yes. Shoot," Ms. Newberry said. She had taken the pliers from Viv and put her head almost entirely inside the dinosaur neck, reaching with her hands for something inside.

"So I'm proposing a new club for next year . . ." Cam began.

"Mm-hmm." Ms. Newberry's response was muffled.

"It's for people who like to make and code. There's not really a space to do that right now, so this club would provide one and also maybe drive up the numbers in the computer science course. And diversify it, of course."

"A worthy goal," Ms. Newberry said. "Don't students have access to the design lab for that?"

Cam looked at Viv. She had been nervous about this sort of pushback, and they had practiced.

Come on! Viv mouthed.

"Yes," Cam said. "But the trouble is that students can access it only if their teachers bring them for a project, and most teachers don't. There's no time for students to freely work on new ideas. The only club that can use the space right now is

RoboSub, and that's a pretty, well, male-heavy team. As you know, Viv and I are the only two girls."

"I see," Ms. Newberry said. "And how does the RoboSub team feel about sharing that space during club time?"

"That's the thing," Cam said, sitting on a stool. "I think it would be better if we used somewhere different. Like, maybe this studio?"

"Got it!" Ms. Newberry said.

Cam and Viv heard a wire snap. Ms. Newberry extracted herself from the dinosaur and turned to face them.

"Finally," she said. "That was really bothering me. So you'd like to host a club in my studio. I think it's a tremendous idea. How can I help?"

Cam smiled. "Awesome! That would be so great. Thank you so much!" She looked at Viv, who shot her a look that said to ask the next thing. "We also need a faculty advisor," Cam went on. "And we hope that could maybe be you."

"Hmm," Ms. Newberry said. "I don't know the first thing about coding, to be honest."

"That's okay!" Cam rushed to say. "The club would be about making too, and the whole point is that we want to expose people to coding who haven't done it before. They just need a safe place and encouragement. I think it's great that you don't know how to code. That could show students that the club is for all types of people."

Ms. Newberry looked impressed. "I can see you've given this a lot of thought."

"It's pretty much all she thinks about right now," Viv chimed in.

Ms. Newberry smiled. "Then I'd love to help. I'm not sure what I can provide beyond this space, my presence, and an occasional vegan snack, but I'm happy to be the advisor."

"That's amazing!" Cam gushed.

"Thanks, Ms. Newberry. That's really cool," Viv added.

"No problem, ladies. Now, if you'll excuse me, I have a date with my couch for the next two weeks."

They said goodbye and left the studio.

"Wow. I really didn't think that would be so easy," Cam said.

"Why? You have a good plan, and you're, like, really nice and smart. Teachers love you. Of course she wanted to help," Viv said.

"I guess I'm just used to the reactions I get in CS and Robo-Sub. I assumed there would be pushback or something."

"Hey," Viv said, turning to her. "Don't get like that."

"Like what?"

"Don't think that things are going to be hard or weird or any sort of way because of how those jerks treat you. If they get in your head, then they get exactly what they want."

Cam nodded. "Yeah. You're right. I'm sorry."

"No apologies," Viv said, straightening up. "Now, let's get moving. We have an entire season of *Grey's Anatomy* to watch before I board a plane to Aruba tomorrow."

```
(function imposter(){
    console.log("Chapter");
    console.log("Fourteen");
})();
```

Chapter Fourteen

Spring break dragged. The days without Vivian were long, slow, and boring. Cam was grateful for break, but her social options were pretty much her parents and ... her parents.

Cam logged into Battle.net to see if Jackson was around.

To her surprise, his handle showed the offline marker. *Oh yeah, he's visiting his sister in California*, she thought.

She lay back on her bed, watching the sunlight make shadows around the room. *Well, this is entertainment rock bottom*, she thought. Just then, her phone pinged. An email.

> Subject: Hey electrical team!
> From: Liam Kensington <lkensington@MacArthurHSOH.edu>
> To: Cameron Goldberg <cgoldberg@MacArthurHSOH.edu>,
> Greg Lowry <glowry@MacArthurHSOH.edu>,
> Jeffrey Neelson <jneelson@MacArthurHSOH.edu>

> Sup Robofam!
> I was thinkin, I'm around for spring break and I'm getting a little tired of playing parcheesi with my grandma. Anyone down for a RoboSesh at my house tonight? 8 pm? See ya there!

Cam sat up in bed and texted Vivian. **SOS. Need phone call as soon as possible. Meeting at Liam's house. Highest priority. Threat level alpha.** Hopefully that would get her attention.

The thought of going to Liam's house made Cam really nervous. *Why?* she wondered. *The other electrical guys will be there too.*

Just as she spiraled into her thoughts, Viv called.

"Ohmigod! This is happening!" Viv screeched into the phone.

Cam had to move the earpiece away from her head. "So you think I should go?"

"*Obviously* I think you should go. I'm standing on an outdoor end table so I can get the only bar of service to tell you that you are definitely going to this hang!"

"I don't know who else will be there."

"Who cares! *Liam* will be there."

Cam laughed.

"I can't believe I'm missing this opportunity," Viv went on.

"Um. Only the electrical team was invited," Cam said.

"Oh, I know. I meant I can't believe I'm missing coming over for a makeover before you go! Seriously. This is like a major best-friend moment, and I'm trapped in an island paradise. Do you need me? You just say the word, and I'll start swimming."

"To Ohio?"

"Friendship finds a way, Cam!"

"I don't think I'm going to dress up. I'll just tell him I'm coming and go over."

"This is exactly the problem. Cam, I love you, but you don't know a perfect makeover opportunity when you see one."

Cam rolled her eyes. "I guess not."

"How are you going to get there?" Viv asked. "Oh god. Your parents can't drive you to a guy's house. I cannot think of anything less cool."

"I don't know. I'm not sure where he lives."

Her phone pinged again. Another email.

Subject: Re: Hey electrical team!
From: Liam Kensington <lkensington@MacArthurHSOH.edu>
To: Cameron Goldberg <cgoldberg@MacArthurHSOH.edu>,
Greg Lowry <glowry@MacArthurHSOH.edu>,
Jeffrey Neelson <jneelson@MacArthurHSOH.edu>

Totally forgot my address 🙈
397 Sycamore Ave
Let me know if you're comin so my mom can get appropriate snackage.

"Another email with his address in it. Hold on." Cam looked it up. It was maybe a mile away. "I can bike it."

"Excellent," Viv replied. "Just make sure you don't get helmet hair. Or wind hair. Just be really mindful of your hair, okay? We both know you have humidity problems."

"Don't worry. I'm not trying to unleash the kraken tonight."

"Listen, I gotta go," Viv said. "Don't wimp out. You are the first to be invited to a junior's house. A cute junior who is single and nice. And did I mention cute?"

"What happened to waiting for college?" Cam asked.

"Opportunity is in your lap, my friend. I'm living vicariously through you, so if you blow it, you're blowing it for me too."

"Okay, okay. I won't bail. Don't worry!" Cam said. "How should I fill you in after?"

"If I start hitchhiking now, I can maybe get there in time," Viv joked. "Just text," she went on. "I'll tape my phone to the corner of this outer wall for service and turn the ringer all the way up so I hear it. Don't worry. I'll be available to debrief."

Cam laughed at the thought of Viv taping her phone to a wall in Aruba.

"Okay! I'll text you later," Cam said.

"Text me constantly!" Viv said, and then the line went dead.

Oh, shit. Cam thought. *I forgot about responding to the email.* She tried Viv but it went straight to voice mail.

She hit Reply All.

Subject: Re: Hey electrical team!
From: Cameron Goldberg <cgoldberg@MacArthurHSOH.edu>
To: Liam Kensington <lkensington@MacArthurHSOH.edu>,
Greg Lowry <glowry@MacArthurHSOH.edu>,
Jeffrey Neelson <jneelson@MacArthurHSOH.edu>

Haha, my grandma loves parcheesi too!

She scrunched up her nose and erased that. *Don't be a weirdo*, she thought, and started again.

Only if there's pizza bites!

That one she considered for a few seconds, then thought better of it.

What would Vivian say in this situation? *Don't play all your cards yet*, Cam imagined her friend saying. *Save that for the real show tonight.*

I'm in! Let me know if I can bring anything.

She hit Send, closed out email, and headed downstairs. Time to tell her parents.

"Hey, guys," she said as she entered the kitchen.

Her mom was wiping down the counter, and her dad was flipping through a cookbook, probably for dinner ideas.

"What's up?" Mom asked. She had just started turning carimañolas on the stove.

"So a bunch of RoboSub people are getting together tonight at Liam's house. At eight. I can bike there, 'cause it's just over on Sycamore. Wanted to let you know!" Cam said. She turned to make an escape.

"Hey. Hold up there, Cam," her dad said, looking up from the cookbook. "Tell us more about this get-together before you scoot off. Remind me who this Liam fellow is?"

"He's the electrical team lead," Cam said.

"A sophomore like you?" her mom asked.

"A junior," she told them. Her parents exchanged a quick look.

"Will his parents be home?" Dad asked.

"I don't know. I think so. He mentioned his mom getting snacks, so . . ." *This is excruciating*, she thought.

"Who else will be there?" Mom asked.

"I'm not sure. He invited the whole electrical team. There are three of us, plus Liam."

Cam knew her parents trusted her, and she knew the questions weren't really about her.

"All right. We'll allow it. But text me the address," Dad said.

"Cool." Cam started walking away.

"And be home by midnight!" he called as she neared the stairs.

She stopped to listen and heard him say quietly, "That's a thing, right? When a teen goes to a boy's house? Is midnight too early?"

Cam heard her mother laugh and knew they weren't too worried about the situation. Luckily they hadn't pushed too hard about Liam. She wasn't good at hiding her feelings, and they could always read her face. It wasn't like anything was going on between her and Liam (as much as Viv wished there were). But Cam wasn't so sure that she didn't *want* something to go on. Like, she didn't *not* want to see him at RoboSub every week. Her stomach hadn't *not* twisted up when she got the email. And she definitely hadn't *not* searched the American Eagle website one night to figure out which cologne he used.

Yikes, she thought. *Keep it together, Cam.*

At quarter to eight Cam was contemplating her appearance in front of her bedroom mirror. She pulled her hair back into a casual ponytail that she hoped would withstand the bike ride. Despite Viv's advice, it freaked Cam out to think about riding her bike without a helmet, and she figured a low pony would stay intact. She wasn't someone who wore a ton of makeup, and she didn't want it to seem like she'd gone above and beyond for this very casual hang. So she applied the same makeup she did for school—tinted moisturizer, a little eyeliner, and cherry ChapStick. Her mother's Panamanian heritage had gifted Cam with thick, dark eyelashes, so she didn't do much work there. Viv was always trying to get her to pluck her eyebrows, and of course Mom had given her the tweezers for Hanukkah. But big eyebrows were in, and Cam didn't like how plucking made her eyes tear up.

She kept her outfit simple—jeans and a T-shirt with a light-weight cardigan. Viv had texted only one thing since they'd talked: **Don't wear a freaking cardigan!** But what could Cam say? She was who she was.

Grabbing her laptop, she raced down the stairs and yelled a quick "See you later!" to her parents, rushing out the door before they could respond. Her mom had boxed up some carimañolas for her to bring to Liam's, and she'd carefully slid them into her backpack.

As she was mounting her bike, she saw her dad trying to peek discreetly through the curtains. She saw his mouth move, probably telling her mom what Cam was wearing. Her mother was smart, so she might be able to tell how Cam felt simply by what Cam had on. Hopefully Cam had played it cool enough to throw her off the scent.

It took only fifteen minutes to bike to Liam's house, and it was 8:02 when she reached his driveway. *Too early*, she thought. She didn't go to many houses other than Viv's, and it never mattered what time she showed up there. She really had no idea what time was cool to arrive. She didn't want to be first. She didn't see any cars parked in the driveway or on the street, which meant the other guys weren't there yet, if they were coming. She wheeled her bike just around the corner and watched for someone to arrive.

After ten minutes she was starting to get bored (and worried that maybe she had the wrong house), when an old sedan pulled into the driveway. Greg got out of the car and went to the front door. Cam's anxiety about being too early was starting to be replaced by anxiety that she was late, so she rode her bike up the driveway and leaned it against the garage. She stashed her helmet and approached the house. Liam opened almost right away. Her stomach did a little jump.

"Hey, Cam! Come on in!" Liam said, stepping aside so she could enter.

"We're down in the basement," he said, leading the way. "How's it goin'?"

"Good, thanks. Um, my mom made carimañolas," she said, holding out the box. "They're kinda like dumplings. They're really good."

"Cool!" he said, opening the box. "Wow! These smell amazing. I've never heard of these."

Cam laughed. "Yeah. She's from Panama. And her cooking is pretty awesome."

"Very cool," Liam said, leading her through the house. "You and Viv up to no good over break?"

She loved that he knew Viv was her best friend. Although he didn't really see Cam other than in RoboSub, so maybe he was just asking about the only friend he knew she had. *Or maybe he's noticing you for other reasons*, she heard Viv's voice quip in her mind.

"Nope. She's in Aruba," Cam said.

"Bummer. Well, not for her, I guess," Liam said as they entered the basement. "Welcome to *mi casa*." He looked back at her. "Oh, sorry. I didn't mean to be, like, rude about Spanish or anything."

Cam didn't know how to take that. Just because her mom was Panamanian didn't mean she owned Spanish or something.

"You know, like inappropriate or whatever," Liam added with a bashful smile.

"It's fine," Cam said, smiling back. "I give you permission to use Spanish." She made the sign of a cross over him. *Way to take that too far*, she thought. But he laughed.

"Not much here, but we keep a fridge through that door stocked with soda and snacks, and there's plenty of space for us to do some work on the sub. I took some soldering irons and stuff home over the break."

"Whoa. I didn't realize we could do that!" Cam said.

"We're supposed to go through a whole process," Liam replied. "But I just kinda did it."

Greg walked through the door and cracked open a Mountain Dew. "Hey, Cam," he said. Greg was pretty innocuous, as far as guys at RoboSub went. He seemed happy to let Cam do her thing and pretty much stuck to himself. He wasn't in CS class, and she'd heard he was kind of a mechanical engineering whiz. He had a scholarship to MIT lined up for next year.

The doorbell rang. "That must be Jeff!" Liam said, and bounded back up the stairs.

That left Cam alone with Greg. "So, how's your break going?" she asked.

He took a sip of soda. "Oh, yeah. It's fine. My sister's home from college. She always gives me hell. Wants to talk about drama at school and stuff—all this girl crap, you know." He took another sip and then realized what he'd said. "Oh! No offense. You know what I mean."

"Um, sure," she said. She did kind of take offense.

"Let's get to work!" Liam said, returning with Jeff. "I've got two irons, and the cabling I brought is in that bin. Thought we could streamline some connections and do some cable management to make things less messy. What do you think?"

"Sounds good," Cam said.

The others agreed.

Liam smiled. "Cool. Let's do it."

< br >

Cam and Liam leaned over the sub, talking about how they might bunch things together and tie them off to reduce clutter.

"In theory we could weld these to the side, and that might allow us to create another layer of water protection for this board," he said, using a tool to point out which wires he meant.

"Cool. This board?" she asked.

He reached over and moved her finger so it pointed to the right cable. "That one," he said.

Her breath caught when he touched her. She fake coughed and leaned away to grab a drink of soda.

"Maybe if we put a pass-through here." She tried to indicate the area she was talking about, but it was buried behind other parts.

"Here?" He pointed to the wrong part.

"No. Um . . ." She glanced around, looking for a tool she could use to lift the wiring so he could see better.

"Just a sec," Liam said, and reached over to the table behind her. He practically had his arm around her. "Here," Liam said, offering her a screwdriver.

Had he noticed how close they were? Did he care?

"Thanks," she said, catching a hint of his cologne. "This is the part I meant." She used the screwdriver to move some cabling aside.

"Gotcha. That's a great idea, Cam. I think we should do it."

"Awesome. Thanks," she said as she turned to look at him.

Their faces were really, really close together. Perhaps closer than Cam had ever been to a boy. She fought the urge to crane her head away. *Is my breath okay?* Were they looking longer than needed or was she imagining it? From this close, she could see his brown eyes had little flecks of green.

"Hey, Liam, check this out," Greg called, waving at them. "I figured out how to make this connection tighter."

Liam smiled at Cam then turned away. "Nice, let's see it."

< br >

A few hours later they were all getting ready to leave. While they were packing up, Liam quietly asked Cam, "Hey, do you want to take one of the soldering irons home?"

"Really? Aren't you using them?"

"I don't need two. And if we get together again, you can always bring it back."

"Cool," Cam said, feeling truly grateful. "I'd love that."

"Great," he said, hands in his pockets.

Did he look at her for too long again? Cam packed up the iron and some solder and joined everyone at the front door.

"See ya, man," Greg said.

Jeff waved goodbye.

"Thank for having us," Cam said.

Liam leaned against the doorframe. "Yeah. Thanks for

coming! Lots of good work. We're gonna crush the competition this year."

"I can't remember if I ever heard how the team did last year," Cam said.

"Pretty much last place," he said. "But we were still figuring out how the whole thing works. It was exciting just to be there, you know?"

"Totally," Cam said. "I'm sure we'll do better than last place this year."

He laughed and nodded. "I hope so. Have a good night."

"Yeah, you too," she said.

When she got to her bike, she realized that riding home with the extra equipment would be tricky. But she managed to balance the box on her handlebars and made it home by 11:30. Her parents were in the living room watching TV.

"How was it?" her dad asked. "Make good progress on the sub?"

"We did, actually," she said. "Liam loaned me some stuff so I can practice." She gestured at the box. "Good night!"

In her room Cam dropped everything on the bed and pulled out her phone. She promised Viv she'd text, and if she knew Viv, she'd been waiting on that porch in Aruba all night. She decided to call instead. Viv picked up on the first ring. "Oh, thank god it's you. My parents are starting to think I made up waiting for you as a way to get away from them."

"How long have you been waiting?" Cam asked.

"Two hours. It's no big deal," Viv said. "Trust me, they're not *totally* wrong about the excuse thing."

"How's it going down there, by the way?" Cam couldn't imagine what it must be like cooped up with Viv's parents like that. *Yikes.*

"Oh, you know, excruciating," Viv said. "Nothing I didn't expect. But who cares about me? Tell me about your night. I need all the tea."

"So I got there a little early—" Cam started.

"No, no! What did you wear? How did you do your hair? Did you wear the helmet? Take me *allll* the way back."

Cam laughed, then walked Viv through the whole night. She purposely delivered the play-by-play in a straightforward way with no embellishments, withholding the info she knew Vivian wanted most.

"That's it?" Viv asked at the end. "No highlights?"

"Well, I *did* have a weird moment when Liam reached around me to get a screwdriver. I could smell his cologne again," Cam said. Viv was fully aware of the first cologne incident.

Viv squealed. "Ohmigod, that is such a classic move. Totally wanted to get closer to you."

Cam laughed. "And after that he kinda looked at me for too long, you know? Like in a movie."

Viv squealed so loud a dog barked in the background. Cam heard someone yell something. "Sorry!" Viv shouted to the stranger. "Cam, I knew it. He totally likes you! This is *so* happening."

"And he asked me if I wanted to take a soldering iron home," Cam went on, starting to believe Viv. Maybe something actually was happening.

"Cute, cute. Trying to support your creative and academic endeavors. Love that." Cam loved it too. "Will you see him again over break?"

"I don't know. He said the group might get together again, but we'll see."

"Cam! You have to take control of this situation. Take initiative."

"What do you mean?"

"You should totally ask him if he wants to hang out."

"No way!" Cam said. That felt too forward, and besides, she could've imagined the attraction between her and Liam.

"Ugh, fine. I can work with this," Viv said, almost to herself. "You should thank him for having you over."

"I did!" Cam said. She wasn't a *total* social shut-in.

"No. I mean use the invitation email as an opportunity to write him again. Have a back-and-forth, you know?"

"Oh! Like email him a thank-you?"

"Yeah. And, like, make it clear it was really fun and you'd be open to hanging out again if he wants. Pull up the email, and we can draft it together."

Subject: Re: Hey electrical team!
From: Cameron Goldberg <cgoldberg@MacArthurHSOH.edu>
To: Liam Kensington <lkensington@MacArthurHSOH.edu>

Hey Liam,
Just wanted to thank you again for organizing the work hang tonight! I had a really good time. I'll be around the rest of break, so let me know if you want to do some more work on the sub. Or if you just want to hang out sometime.
See ya, Cam

Viv wanted her to add a blushing smiley emoji, but Cam said no way.

"What if he *does* want to hang out again over break?" Cam asked.

"What do you mean? That would be great!"

"If we hang out alone, I feel like I might literally puke on him."

Viv laughed. "You would not. And I think that's a good feeling to have."

"Okay. I'm sending it," Cam said.

"Woo!" Viv shouted.

Her computer swooshed, indicating the message had gone. She had emailed a boy, offering to hang out.

"You really need to get back before he responds so you can help me with this," Cam said.

"Ugh. Don't tempt me, girl. You know I might just make a run for it at any minute."

They got lost talking about other things (Viv's Aruba highlights, Cam's progress on her CS project). Then Cam heard a notification sound from her laptop. New email.

"Ohmigod," she said. "He already wrote back."

"Ohmigod!" Viv shouted. "Open it! Read it!"

"Okay, okay. One sec," Cam said. She read the email to Viv.

Subject: Re: Hey electrical team!
From: Liam Kensington <lkensington@MacArthurHSOH.edu>
To: Cameron Goldberg <cgoldberg@MacArthurHSOH.edu>

Hey,
Yeah, thanks for coming! And thanks for being so committed to RoboSub 🙂 My family is leaving for a trip the rest of break, but I'm hoping to get some more work done the weekend we get back, before school starts. Here's my number in case you have any questions about soldering or whatever: 220-555-0198 Liam

Viv broke the stunned silence. "Oh. My. God."

"I know."

"He gave you his number."

"I know."

"A cute junior who smells nice gave you his number!"

"He did," Cam said, grinning wider than she ever had, her heart fluttering wildly in her chest. Cam Goldberg had gotten a number. Oh, how times were changing.

"You should text him," Viv said.

"I can't do that right now. He'll think I'm a weirdo! Or desperate. He just sent this message like three minutes ago."

"Okay. Fair. But you should use this as an opening to text him so he has your number. That's how number sharing works," Viv said.

"Okay. I'll do that in the morning."

"What if he's not available in the morning because he already left on vacation? He didn't say where he was going. It could be out of the country!"

"You're out of the country. And iMessage will still work," Cam said.

"What if he doesn't have iMessage?"

"I saw his phone. He does," Cam replied. "Don't worry, I'll get him my number!"

Viv sighed. "Okay. Fine. But keep me updated. And don't wimp out! Just ask, 'What would Viv do next?'"

"Yeah, and then tone it down by seventy-five percent and do that," Cam said, laughing.

```
(function imposter(){
    console.log("Chapter");
    console.log("Fifteen");
})();
```

Chapter Fifteen

Cam spent the rest of the week practicing with the soldering iron and some old Arduino boards she'd taken ages ago from the design lab junk box. She'd texted Liam a simple message that said, **Hey, it's Cam** so he'd have her number. He'd responded with a wave emoji.

I won't wimp out, she reminded herself. *I'm just waiting until I have something to say.*

Without much else to distract her, she threw herself into the prototyping for her and Jackson's CS project. The presentation was only a month away, and Cam was starting to feel anxious. The game itself was coming along: they'd completed most of the code and were debugging and finalizing the artwork. Cam had learned an incredible amount about game design. It was sort of unimaginable now how little she knew just a few short months ago.

Her report on their problem was nearly done as well. The data spoke for itself. It wasn't hard to imagine why girls and women dropped out of classes and careers at staggering rates. She'd spoken to Viv about it the night before.

"Well, of course there's not just, like, some magic thing to end it," Viv had said. "It's systemic."

"But how do we create systemic change? That feels . . . I don't know . . . impossible," Cam replied.

"Not impossible. But pretty messy, I think. Just look at the civil rights movement. People were beaten in the streets, and they passed all this legislation and stuff, but people still need Black Lives Matter, and it feels like the same exact bullshit, you know?"

"I don't even know where to start."

"You already did. Caring is the first step. You care, and then you find other folks who care, and then you grow it from there. I think it *really* gets hard when you start demanding people do something about it."

That was why Cam was stuck on how to end her paper. She knew exactly what she wanted to say, exactly what she wanted the school to do. It was a small step to establish a way for girls to make and code. But it was still *something*—to ask for something. Action felt risky. What if they said no? What if she made a case and did all this work and nobody cared?

She took a breath and closed her eyes. Reshma Saujani had mentioned this feeling. It was how girls were trained to feel: so afraid of failure that they avoided risks. Cam committed again to fighting that feeling. Committed to trying. And if she failed, she'd just have to try again.

< br >

Cam was listening to music and looking over code when her bedroom door burst open.

"I'm back!" Viv said, brandishing a bag of goodies from Aruba.

Cam cheered and jumped up to hug her. "What did you bring me?" she asked, reaching for the bag.

"Well, let's see. We got coffee; we got sand in a bottle; we got chocolate; we got this lizard art." Viv tossed each item on to the bed as she named it. "And the return of the best friend!"

"I'm so glad you're back," Cam said, opening some chocolate and taking a bite. "Wow. That's good."

"So tell me, is Liam back? Have you made contact?"

"That's all you want to know?"

"Oh, no, you're right. How's your project going?" Viv asked.

"Well—" Cam began.

"Girl, no. I don't wanna hear about that! I wanna hear about the love interest! Do you know me at all?" She grabbed the chocolate and broke off a piece.

Cam laughed. "Honestly, I haven't texted him. I just gave him my number."

"Let's do it right now!" Viv said, reaching for Cam's phone.

Cam held it away from her. "I don't have anything to say!"

"No one ever has nothing to say. Just ask him . . . I don't know . . . ask him how his trip was."

Cam thought, then unlocked her phone. She typed: **Hey! How was the trip with fam?**

"I feel weird sending this," she said.

"Why?"

"Because we don't have a relationship! I don't know him! Why would I ask about his family?"

"You have to start somewhere," Viv said. She had a point.

Cam sent the text. She and Viv watched some Netflix. Cam's phone buzzed fifteen minutes later. **It was great! You know, typical drama between the olds about who pays for dinner, what we eat for dinner, and pretty much all dinner logistics every day** 😊

Cam nudged Viv and showed her.

"Oh, that's funny! He's funny. Write him back," she said.

Cam typed: **LOL. I wonder if we'll hit an age where all we can think about is paying for dinner and if it should be tacos or pizza.**

"That's good. That's funny," Viv said.

They went back to Netflix but had hardly hit play when Cam's phone buzzed again. **This is one of my greatest fears** 😉

Cam wrote back: **Are you excited for RoboSub to start back up?**

Three dots showed he was typing. **Totally! This is really crunch time.**

She replied. **Agree! Like I can hear my dad saying "The early bird gets the worm, Cammie!"**

As soon as she hit Send, she felt her stomach drop. She glanced at Viv.

"What?" Viv said.

"I just quoted my dad."

"Why?" Viv asked with a laugh.

"I don't know! I was shooting from the hip. It just came out!"

"Let me see," Viv said, pulling at the phone. "Oh, geez. You gave dad advice."

"I did do that."

"Oh, but he's typing again!"

They peered at the phone, faces smushed in close. **My dad says that too! Maybe there's something to it hahaha**

Viv sat up and fanned herself. "Oooh, this boy is sending you emojis left and right. He *likes* you."

Cam blushed. "I don't know."

Viv picked up a pillow and tossed it at her. "He likes you."

"I feel like I might vomit."

"Then you're doing it right!" Viv said. And they both laughed.

< br >

Cam was weirdly excited for school to start again. Home was boring, and the last months of school were always fast, with lots of events to wrap up the year.

In late April, Viv went to Orlando for the big DECA ICDC to compete and do the live-judge component for her project. Cam missed her, but was also sort of grateful to be without distractions during crunch time for the CS project.

"I think we should practice our presentation on Friday," Cam said to Jackson.

The presentations were in two weeks. Each group had twenty minutes. It would take up a whole week of class. Mr. Lenox would grade them based on their written report, the presentation, and how well they handled questions.

"Cool with me," Jackson said.

"Do you think we'll have the game final by then?"

"Pretty much." Something seemed strange with him. "I just need to add the music."

"Cool," she said, trying to put her finger on what was off.

He dipped a fry in ketchup and it hit her: He wasn't on his computer. He was just sitting there eating fries and talking. No screen between them, no eyes rapidly moving around, no hands flying over a keyboard. It was so . . . different.

"When do you think we'll book flights and stuff for RoboSub?" Cam asked.

Jackson shrugged.

"I can't wait to meet other teams," Cam said.

"Aren't they, like, mostly colleges?" Jackson asked.

"Yep. There might be only a few high schools there."

"Seems like we don't have much shot of winning," he replied.

"Oh, we have no shot," Cam said with a laugh. "I'll be pumped if we complete the course and make it out of trials."

"Jeremy will be so pissed if we can't complete the course. I can see him, like, having a fit right on the TRANSDEC," Jackson said, grinning.

Cam's phone buzzed with a FaceTime from Viv.

"Hey! How'd it go?" Cam asked. Viv's interview was earlier that afternoon, and Cam hadn't heard from her all day.

Viv was surrounded by a sea of teens in blue blazers like hers. She clutched a glass trophy that she squeezed next to her face. "I won!"

"Ohmigod!" Cam screamed, startling Jackson. "She won!"

"I can tell," he said. He leaned over and said, "Congrats, Viv."

Viv squealed. "I was so nervous. My judge was so hard to read, so I was like, 'I am totally bombing this,' but your girl pulled it out!"

Someone called to her from off-screen.

"I gotta go. There's a chapter meeting now and an after-party later. I'll be back tomorrow!"

"Congratulations again!" Cam said. She was so happy for Viv. *At least one of our presentations went well*, she thought. *My turn next.*

```
(function imposter(){
    console.log("Chapter");
    console.log("Sixteen");
})();
```

Chapter Sixteen

Presentation day arrived. Cam and Jackson were scheduled second on day two. Cam felt ready. She would discuss the research and the inspiration for the game, and Jackson would do a walkthrough. They would divide the questions, and she'd even printed their report and put it into one of those plastic report-cover things her mom was always trying to get her to use. Cam was determined to do well. They were going to crush it.

Two teams presented on day one, and Cam was not very impressed. Both had proposed apps that solved issues of personal inconvenience. The data supporting their projects was mostly friend surveys. Cam glanced at Mr. Lenox's face during each presentation, but he was hard to read. The questions students asked weren't serious, so Cam didn't know how Mr. Lenox could accurately figure that part of the grade.

Trying to be discreet, Cam looked over her notes as the current group finished up. Jackson was totally calm and seemed unconcerned about the outcome, but she'd come to expect that. For her this was a big deal.

Finally everyone clapped for the first presentation, and Mr. Lenox called Cam and Jackson to the front. Jackson hooked up his computer to the screen, and Cam looked out at the all-male audience.

When she practiced, she didn't think about what it would feel like to stand in front of a group as the only girl. Nausea hit her, and she took a deep breath while willing herself not to blush. Most of the boys stared blankly at the screen, waiting for them to start. Jeremy smirked, but she had to ignore that. Her eyes rested on Matt, who looked straight at her and smiled. His encouraging nod shored her up. She swallowed and began.

"The computer science industry in this country has been plagued since its inception with systemic misogyny that permeates all levels, even to this day." Her dad helped her with that line. Cam went on to talk about the myths of "the pipeline," achievement gaps, and the supposed lack of interest girls had in coding. Everything she said had research to support it, and she felt brave. Her unease faded away as she built toward the harder stuff: microaggressions, discrimination, walkouts, and lawsuits. Their classmates' faces stayed mostly blank, but it didn't matter. When Cam finished defining the problem, Jackson took over and explained the game, how it could make money, and how the research informed their design choices. As he flipped through the different screens, Cam passed around the prototypes she'd made.

When the stapler-turned-weapon got to Jeremy, he let it drop to the floor with a loud clatter, which interrupted Jackson.

"Oops, sorry," Jeremy said.

Jackson waited for the snickers to pass. He held the silence for a little too long—long enough for Jeremy to get uncomfortable and look down.

When Jackson finished, Cam outlined the idea for a club at their school. She talked about how the money raised from game sales would fund materials. When she finished there was silence.

It made Mr. Lenox look up from his notes. "Questions?"

Jeremy's hand went up.

"Mr. Woburn," Mr. Lenox said.

"Yeah. Isn't your club unfair?"

Jackson stood beside Cam. "Unfair how?" he asked.

"Because it excludes male students. There aren't any clubs that exclude female students, so why is it okay to exclude male students?"

Cam spoke up. "The research clearly shows that girls need social environments where they can thrive, away from the microaggression and discrimination they face in spaces with boys. And it's not exclusive. Girls Who Code national specifically says that. Their programming is girls-focused, but any gender identity is welcome to join. You just need to believe in the mission of creating safe spaces for girls."

"Well, why can't there be spaces only for boys, then, if there are spaces for girls?"

"All spaces are for boys," Cam countered. "That's the whole point."

There were some *oohs* from the other boys.

Jeremy's face flushed. His hand went up again.

"Yes, Mr. Woburn?" Mr. Lenox said.

"I find your game offensive."

"Offensive how?" Jackson asked.

"It depicts men as weird monsters with big hands and mouths. It's rude. It's like, you know, like those cartoon drawings with big heads."

"A caricature?" Matt asked. He had turned in his chair to look at Jeremy.

"Right. It's a caricature! I'm personally offended," Jeremy said, crossing his arms and sitting back in his chair.

Matt rolled his eyes. "It's not a caricature of *you*, Jeremy. Come on."

Jeremy shot him a look.

If looks could kill, Cam thought. "I'm sure you've noticed that women in video games are hypersexualized—"

Jeremy interrupted her. "I don't feel comfortable in this class anymore." A light gleamed in his eye. His voice was smug.

A few boys chuckled, thinking he was kidding.

"Or safe," Jeremy added. "I don't feel *safe* in this class."

That must've been a trigger word for Mr. Lenox because he closed his notes and stood up. "All right, that's enough from these presenters. Thank you. Please have a seat."

No one had asked Cam or Jackson a real question about their ideas, and now no one could. Their question time was maybe sixty seconds, and Jeremy used it all up with his taunts. Other teams had answered questions for at least a few minutes.

Cam asked to be excused to the bathroom. She stood in front of the sinks and took some deep breaths. *What just happened?*

The door opened and Jackson came in, looking around nervously.

"Jackson? This is the girls' bathroom," she said.

"I know," he said. "No one's in here, right?"

"No. No one but me."

He relaxed. "Good. Listen. I think we did a great job. Jeremy's questions were bullshit."

"Do you think so?" she asked. "I mean, he's obviously wrong, but the way Mr. Lenox reacted—"

"Lenox is useless. He probably just didn't know how to deal, so he shut it down."

"But what happens to our grade? We didn't really get to do the question requirement."

"Lenox is so lazy. I bet he skims the reports and gives us all an A."

"Do you really think so?" Tears formed in Cam's eyes. The stress of possibly doing poorly after all the work, because Jeremy sabotaged yet another thing, coursed through her body.

"Yeah, I do." Jackson took a step closer. "Hey, listen. We crushed it. The other projects are literally so pointless. They don't fix problems. You worked really hard, Cam. We made a great project."

His words pushed her over the edge. All the stress she'd been carrying—about the project, the presentation, RoboSub, Jeremy—rushed out in a burst. Without thinking, she collapsed into Jackson. He stiffened, put his arms around her, and patted her back.

"I'm sorry. It's just been a lot. It's so nice to hear you say all that," she said, her tears dampening his shoulder.

"That's okay," he said, hands fumbling. "That's okay."

She got herself together and pulled back. She wiped her face with a paper towel. "Sorry about that," she said, laughing slightly. "I don't know what happened to me."

"There's nothing to be sorry about," he said. "Come on. Let's go get our stuff."

< br >

That night at dinner, Cam's parents asked about the presentation. Cam told them the truth—she had no idea what their grade would be.

"When will you have the teacher's feedback?" Mom asked.

Cam shrugged. "Probably next week."

After moving a meatball around her plate a few times, she excused herself and went upstairs. There was a sinking feeling in her stomach. They did a good job and fulfilled all the requirements. They deserved a good grade—on the project and in the class. But something about Jeremy's smirk still haunted her.

The next day, as CS class wound down after two more presentations, Mr. Lenox spoke as he erased the board. "Ms. Goldberg and Mr. Wentworth, please see me after class for a moment."

Cam shot a glance at Jackson, who actually looked up from his laptop. There was only one reason Lenox would want to speak to them.

"Right," Mr. Lenox said, looking down and shuffling some papers. "I got a complaint about your project being discriminatory. I need time to review it carefully and decide what to do."

Cam's head spun. A complaint? How did a person even file a complaint about a project? What were the parameters for a student project to be considered discriminatory?

"Who complained?" Jackson asked.

"I'm not at liberty to say," Mr. Lenox replied.

"What might happen?" Cam asked. "If you decide the project is discriminatory . . . what's next?"

Mr. Lenox thought for a moment. "I could consider partial credit or it could be a zero."

Cam's face flushed. *A zero. After all that work.*

"Are you kidding right now?" Jackson asked.

"My hands are tied," Mr. Lenox said. "I have to consider the complaint."

"Well, then, can we redo the project?" Jackson asked.

"Oh, no," Mr. Lenox said. "There isn't time at this point in the term."

Jackson drew a deep breath. "How can we pass this class with partial or no credit?"

"It's not possible," Mr. Lenox said, looking somewhat sympathetic.

Cam had felt unsettled ever since Mr. Lenox cut their question time short the day before. But she wouldn't have predicted a zero, or worse, a failed course. The possibility jolted her brain into attack mode. This was more than another stupid joke. This could change her future.

She heard Viv's voice in her head: *Break the wheel.*

Then she heard her mother: *No one's gonna hand anything to women if we keep our heads down.*

"Sir, who can we speak to about this?" she asked.

"Speak to?"

"Yes. Where is the school policy? What options do we have to challenge the complaint?"

Jackson looked impressed.

"Well, I'm sure in the handbook . . ." Mr. Lenox trailed off.

"I'll review that as soon as possible," Cam said. "I'm sure we have options to discuss or challenge the complaint. You just told us you might fail us. Do you understand the effect that will have on our transcripts?"

Mr. Lenox's mouth opened and closed as he struggled for words.

Cam hiked her backpack higher and squared her shoulders. "This isn't finished," she said, and stormed out.

Jackson was hot on her heels. "Whoa. That was cool," he said.

"Thanks."

"He can't fail our project. It's a good project!"

"Of course it is," Cam said. "And I'll give you one guess who complained."

Jackson snorted. "Yep. So what are you going to do?"

"I'm going to get my hands on a handbook," she said. "And then I'm going to fight back."

"Can I help?" he asked.

"Totally," Cam said.

< br >

Cam went straight to her room that night and googled until she found the district's discrimination policy.

It is district policy that no one shall be treated differently, separately, or have any action directly affecting them taken on the basis of race, religion, national origin, marital status, sex, sexual orientation, gender identity, or disability where a person is otherwise qualified or could be with reasonable accommodation. The immediate remedy for any act of discrimination shall be to end it, treat the individual equally, and as much as practically possible, to eradicate any effects of discrimination. Discipline should be imposed where appropriate.

It was vague, but underneath it she found more about harassment.

Punishable harassment is defined as conduct, including verbal conduct, that (1) creates (or will certainly create) a hostile environment by substantially interfering with a student's educational benefits, opportunities, or performance, or with a student's physical or psychological well-being; or (2) is threatening or seriously intimidating.

That certainly didn't describe their project, but it *did* describe the way Jeremy had treated her. Mr. Lenox hadn't done a thing about any of it. Fired up, Cam unplugged her laptop and ran downstairs to share what had happened with her parents. It all came out in a rush, and she watched her mother's eyes grow wide and her father's face turn redder and redder.

"Nena, this is not right. We must do something," her mom said.

"I'm going to call the school. This is ridiculous!" said Dad.

"But I don't think we should talk to Mr. Lenox," Cam said. "I think we should talk to his boss." She'd been thinking about the right approach, and her mom's plan for how to deal with Shane inspired her. Go above the roadblock and get accountability.

"I'll call first thing in the morning," her mom said. "Are you okay to go to school?"

Cam nodded. She wasn't going to let Jeremy shake her that much.

< br >

The next morning Viv met Cam at her locker. "I just can't believe this stuff with Lenox. It's so wild," she said. "It's like people who claim reverse racism—this is reverse sexism. Like, dude, that's not a thing."

"I know," Cam said. "But Lenox is totally ignorant."

"Maybe," Viv said. "Honestly, I'm not so sure. We should report him. Call the newspaper or something."

Cam laughed. "The newspaper? What would they do?"

"I don't know, write about it!" Viv said.

"My parents are calling the school today. We're going to request a meeting with the principal."

"Fingers crossed," Viv said. "And if he doesn't help you, I'm outta here. I don't care what my parents say. I'm transferring to a boarding school or something."

Viv hugged Cam and turned down the hall to class as Cam headed to computer science.

Cam and Jackson were already in their seats when Jeremy entered.

He flashed his familiar smirk when he saw them. "How's everybody doing today?" he asked as he passed.

Cam just glared, determined not to be baited. She hoped Jackson would follow her lead. No such luck.

"You know, Woburn, you're kind of an asshole," Jackson said.

"Excuse me?" Jeremy said, turning toward him.

"Actually, I misspoke," Jackson said. "Woburn, you *are* an asshole. Can you get away from us? Thanks."

Jeremy tilted his head and appeared ready to speak.

But Jackson stuck out a hand. "Nope, that'll be all. You can just proceed to fuck right off. Thanks."

They were starting to attract attention, and Cam knew Jeremy hated nothing more than looking bad in front of the other guys. He gave a fake laugh and sauntered away.

Cam turned to Jackson. *Awesome*, she mouthed.

He smiled and went back to his video game.

< br >

When Cam got home, she was eager for any news from her parents. Mr. Lenox didn't mention anything, and he didn't ask to speak with them again. Her parents had a "no texting at school" rule that meant they wouldn't contact her while she was in class unless there was an emergency. She'd been on edge all day. She ambushed her mom as soon as she walked in the door.

"So? What did the principal say?"

"He's going to meet with us and Jackson's parents tomorrow morning. I talked with Jackson's stepmom."

"Whoa," Cam said. "That's good, right?"

Her mom smiled. "Yes, nena, that's good. You should prepare what you want to say."

That surprised her. "What I want to say?"

"Of course!" Mom replied. "You and Jackson will be at the meeting. The principal asked for that specifically."

"Wait. Are we in trouble?" Going to the principal's office with her parents felt more like discipline than justice.

"Well, right now, I guess so," her mom replied. "This complaint that was made—the principal wants to know more about it. When I called to ask about it, it was news to him. He'll probably ask you questions."

"Whoa. Okay," Cam said, sitting at the counter.

Her mom put her hands on Cam's shoulders. "Nena. Now it's time for *you* to have a say. What do you want?"

What do I want? A mess of thoughts swirled in her head. There was so much she could tell the principal—her experiences in class and RoboSub, how Jeremy treated her all term, all the data about girls and women in the industry, her new club idea—the list felt endless. But she was sure time would be limited, so she had to distill everything down to one message. What would that be?

She had one night to figure it out.

```
(function imposter(){
    console.log("Chapter");
    console.log("Seventeen");
})();
```

Chapter Seventeen

The next morning, Cam couldn't eat. She turned down the coffee her dad offered—she didn't need anything to make her jittery. Her parents were quiet and pretended they weren't watching her, but it was obvious.

Cam avoided her classmates' gazes as she and her parents made their way to the main office. They were shown into Principal Carter's office and sat in a semicircle facing his desk. Jackson was between his parents on the right, and Cam was between her parents on the left. Jackson slumped in his chair. He had on a button-down shirt and pants that fit. His hair was combed, and he was not happy about any of it.

Principal Carter came in and the adults stood up, shook his hand, and introduced themselves. Cam's dad's face was tight and angry—Cam didn't see it like that very often. Her mom looked at Principal Carter with skepticism.

"So we're here to discuss the issue of a final project for Mr. Lenox's Introduction to Computer Science course this spring term." He checked a paper in front of him.

Had he not prepared ahead of time? It was as if he was seeing the information for the first time.

"Mr. Lenox is considering partial credit or a zero due to a complaint from a student in the class."

"Cam and Jackson asked Mr. Lenox if they could redo the project so as not to receive a zero," Cam's dad jumped in. "The project is worth half the semester's grade. If Jackson and Cam are given a zero, they can't pass the class. That type of thing can have a big impact on a transcript when it comes time to apply to college."

Jackson's stepmom nodded.

Principal Carter looked sympathetic. "I understand. I apologize this wasn't brought to my attention sooner. Let's see what we have here." He looked over the notes. "The complaint says the project is offensive because of how it depicts men, and the proposed solution for the problem discussed by the research is discriminatory. A student was personally offended, and when the claim was brought to Mr. Lenox, he found it had merit."

"Offensive? Come on." Jackson spoke, shocking everyone into silence. He sat up straighter. "And we know it was Jeremy Woburn who complained. I sit in that class and listen to those guys trash Cam every day." He nodded at Principal Carter, then gestured to both dads. "You all know it's true. That's what guys do when there aren't many girls around. Or even when there are. Some guys talk bad about girls no matter what, and Jeremy's one of them. Mr. Lenox knows it too. One day I wrote down a bunch of stuff I'd heard Jeremy say and left it on Lenox's desk. He didn't do a thing about it."

Wait. What? Cam thought. *When did he do that?*

Principal Carter sighed and wrote something down.

"We all know Jeremy isn't actually offended by our project," Jackson continued. "We all know when a girl stands up to a mean guy, that guy tries to crush her. We see it all around us. If you're a guy, you can do whatever you want. If you're a girl and you say something, that guy comes back twice as hard, and he brings friends. Guys think they have to be strong and anyone who speaks against them has to be put in their place. That's not strength."

He glanced at Cam, whose mouth was hanging open. That the boys in class had said terrible things about her wasn't a surprise, and she didn't want to know the details. But to know that Jackson left a note for Mr. Lenox and tried to stick up for her. That was so kind it made her want to cry. Jackson nodded at her. It was her turn to speak.

"We did more research to support our project than any other group," she said, putting a large stack of papers on the principal's desk. All their research done over the course of the term. "We met every parameter Mr. Lenox set for us, and unlike the other groups, we addressed a real problem. We could turn money from sales of our game into a direct solution for the problem we researched, just like Mr. Lenox asked."

"What was your proposed solution?" Principal Carter asked, flipping through the pages.

Cam glanced at her father. "A chapter of Girls Who Code at MacArthur."

Principal Carter nodded. "Ah, yes. That was the other part of the complaint. That the club is exclusive and discriminatory on the basis of sex."

Cam sighed. "That's not true. It's for people who want to create safe spaces for female-identifying students. You don't have to be female to want that." She paused.

Mom gave her a supportive nod.

"I saw this meme online of Ruth Bader Ginsburg, and I looked it up. It's a real quote from her. She said that people sometimes ask her when there will be enough women on the Supreme Court, and she always responds, 'When there are nine.' People are surprised, because that would mean no men on the court. But she said, 'There'd been nine men, and nobody's ever raised a question about that.'"

Cam looked up at Principal Carter. "You've never raised a question about why there are so few girls enrolled in CS class." He glanced down. She continued, "You've never raised a question about there being no girls in RoboSub. You've never raised a question about yearly statistics about what majors your graduates would pursue in college. Do you know that Mr. Lenox almost let Jeremy block me and Viv from attending the RoboSub competition this year?"

"I did not know that. No," Principal Carter said. He did not look pleased.

"He said there were too many people, and we needed a female chaperone. Which we found—on our own. That's the thing: Men are automatically supported. For most of human history, most spaces were for men. Men flourish, and it's no surprise. Of course they do." Cam scooted to the edge of her seat. "Women deserve those spaces too. Where we can be together without the anxiety caused by aggression from men who don't want to share access. We are capable, and we have ideas, and we are *good* at things—*really* good. Better than men at a lot of things, actually, according to research." She held up her papers a little. "But it's a lot harder to be creative when you're dealing with a bunch of guys making crude jokes about you in the back of the room."

"I have something to add," Dad said, glancing at Cam. "I know Cam would prefer I don't, but Gabi and I are concerned about this teacher, Mr. Lenox. We don't feel he's supported Cam this term. This stuff with the chaperone and the trip doesn't sit well with me."

"I agree," Mom chimed in. "And I find it unacceptable that your office wasn't aware of this situation with the project. Don't teachers have to report things like this to the administration?"

Principal Carter gave a small nod and sat back in his seat. He looked at all of them. "Well," he said, "you've certainly given me a lot to think about. I'm going to review everything over the weekend. You'll hear from me on Monday."

All the parents thanked him for his time. Cam stood and looked at him. She needed him to understand the culture he was enabling. She desperately wanted everybody in a position of power to understand that. Change can't come from just a few people. What's the point of leadership if they don't take action to make things better? Why bother being a leader at all?

Cam and Jackson left the office without shaking Principal Carter's hand.

"That was cool—what you said," Jackson said, when they were outside the office.

She shrugged. "It was just the truth. I'm tired of tiptoeing around it. Our project is good, Jackson."

"Yeah, it is."

"That was amazing, Cam," Dad said, coming out of the office. "We're really proud of you."

Tears stung her eyes. Standing up to bullies didn't make her cry, but warm words from someone who loved her set her off like a waterfall. "Thanks, Dad."

"No matter what happens, we know you're right, nena," Mom added. "We'll figure out what happens next if we need to. Your father and I will not let this affect your chances at a good college. Don't worry about that." Pulling Cam close, Mom said in her ear, "And I like that boy. Very nice. Head on straight. It's not often you find a good friend like that."

"Yeah, I know," Cam said, glancing over at Jackson, who

was saying goodbye to his parents. Cam realized he'd become just that—a really good friend.

That night Vivian came over and Cam told her the whole thing.

"Wow, your speech was *awesome*," Viv said. "Invoking RBG? Incredible."

"You know that meme with the words over her face?"

"Of course, of course. Iconic."

"Right. When he said the complaint claimed it was discriminatory to have a club for girls, that meme was all I could think about. So I just went with it."

"And Jackson giving that note to Mr. Lenox? Very cool. Even though the jerk didn't do anything about it."

Cam nodded. What Jackson tried to do was really kind.

"What do you think Carter will do?" Viv asked.

"I don't know, but if we don't get full credit, I don't know what *we'll* do. My chance at a college scholarship seems totally shot. My parents think we could do something about it. Put a note in my applications about what happened, but I don't know."

"Any colleges that read that note and don't accept you are fools," Viv said. "It would be their loss."

Maybe. But applying to college was stressful enough. Cam didn't need this hanging over her, constantly making her wonder if she could've done better or if she should've chosen a less hot-button topic.

"Let's watch a movie and eat a bunch of ice cream," Viv said, sitting up and giving Cam's shoulder a little shove. "Enough of this mess. Nothing we can do about it right now, right?"

Cam nodded, but it was a sad nod.

"Come on. For some reason I'm in the mood for late-nineties, early-aughts teen movies with weird hair accessories and Jeeps."

That made Cam laugh. They loved throwback teen movies.

Later that night, after *Bring It On*, *10 Things I Hate About You*, two pints of Ben & Jerrys, and a frozen pizza, Cam tried to fall asleep. She lay there staring up at those little glow-in-the-dark stars on her ceiling. When she was little, she was fascinated by space and wanted to feel like a piece of it was in her bedroom. When had she stopped caring about space so much? She couldn't remember, but based on her research, she imagined it had something to do with how it was presented to her in science classes. Or by the media. All the astronauts on the first moon mission were men. In fact, everyone who had walked on the moon was a man.

Cam felt like she was done cowering from guys who wanted to scare her away. Done letting people convince her she wasn't good enough. Done working so hard to convince herself that they were wrong. They weren't right. Not about her and not about the countless girls and women all over the world, looking up at their own stars and wondering about walking on the moon. They'd never seen it done before, but that didn't mean it couldn't happen. They just needed to fight.

Cam would keep fighting.

```
(function imposter(){
    console.log("Chapter");
    console.log("Eighteen");
})();
```

Chapter Eighteen

The meeting with Principal Carter was at ten Monday morning. Cam's mom broke her own rule and texted to let Cam know that parents weren't coming. Apparently Principal Carter updated them by phone. Cam's mom wouldn't tell her details. She sent a dancing girl emoji.

That's probably a good sign, right? Cam texted Viv.

A few minutes before ten, Cam was waiting outside the principal's office when Jackson came up and took the seat beside her.

"Hey," he said.

"Hey."

"Have a good weekend?"

Small talk from Jackson? He must really be nervous. "Yeah, it was okay."

He nodded. "Cool."

"Ms. Goldberg and Mr. Wentworth, Principal Carter will see you now."

Principal Carter was typing when they entered. "Ms. Goldberg. Mr. Wentworth. Good morning. Have a seat," he said. "I've decided that your project should not be given a zero. Or partial credit."

Cam felt the air rush out of her. She didn't know she'd been holding her breath.

"I instructed Mr. Lenox to evaluate the project per his assignment parameters, using the same rubric by which he graded the other projects. I will personally check it to ensure the grade you receive is fair. From reading your work and the assignment this weekend, I feel confident you've earned a good score."

He went on. "I played the game over the weekend."

Cam and Jackson glanced at each other. *What did he think?*

"I thought it was quite clever," he said, smiling at them. "There are ways in which something like this *could* be offensive if not done well. But you two did it well. If people don't like the reality—well, they should change it."

Cam couldn't believe it. The principal looked at her.

"Regardless of the grade you receive, and regardless of how much funding you can raise from game sales, you may start your club next year, Cam."

"Really?"

"Oh yes," he replied. "I reviewed our graduation records, and it was as you suggested. Female graduates test quite well in math and science, but very few choose to pursue those fields at institutions of higher learning. And our computer science program, while regrettably small, has always served exclusively male students. Perhaps it's time we expand. I'd like it to be more inclusive and inviting to all students. I'm hoping you might be willing to help me think about how to do that."

"Me?" Cam asked. Jackson grinned at her.

"Yes, you," Principal Carter replied. "Who better? You have experienced the programs as they are, and it is clear we're not doing our best."

She didn't know what to say. Luckily Principal Carter went on. He turned to Jackson.

"The response to your note to Mr. Lenox, Mr. Wentworth, was not acceptable based on our policy about reporting bullying. It's also clear that the RoboSub team has been neglected. We've posted that position for the faculty to consider, and I hope someone will volunteer to help the team. You'll need a new advisor for travel to San Diego this summer."

"Ms. Newberry already agreed to come, so we just need one more," Cam said.

Principal Carter considered this. "Excellent. The competition is in July—two months away. I'm sure something will work out between now and then. Finally," he said, turning back to Cam, "I want to apologize to you, Ms. Goldberg. We haven't done our best work in supporting you. We're proud to have such an innovative, intelligent, empathetic young woman in our student body. We have not done enough to encourage you to grow here. I am hoping you will allow *us* to grow for you, and in turn we'll be worthy of such a dedicated member of our community."

Cam felt her face flush. No one had ever given her so much praise, besides her parents.

"Mr. Wentworth, I also want to commend you," Principal Carter said.

"Me?" Jackson said, pointing to his *World of Warcraft* T-shirt-clad chest.

"Yes, you. You stood up for a friend, in more ways than one, I suspect. I know it's difficult to do what you did. I've been in many a locker room and overheard conversations I wish had not taken place. You did something to change it. That bravery has not gone unnoticed."

Jackson's cheeks turned pink, and he shrugged. "Yeah. No big deal."

"Do either of you have any questions for me?" Principal Carter asked, folding his hands on his desk.

"Um, I do have one," Cam said.

"Please," he said.

"Will the rest of the class know? About our project?" Cam thought, *What will Jeremy do? How can I keep working with him on RoboSub?*

"No," Principal Carter said. "The grades of individual students are not the business of anyone else. They will only know if you choose to tell them. But I'm not naïve. Word might spread."

Cam nodded. Everybody knew everybody's business.

"I will meet with the student who made the complaint this afternoon," Principal Carter said. "You've given me some excellent information to share," he said, again gesturing to the papers. "I will encourage the student to do further reading on these issues before raising discriminatory claims in the future."

I'm sure he'll love that, Cam thought.

"Any other questions?" Principal Carter asked.

Cam and Jackson shook their heads.

Principal Carter stood up and reached out to shake their hands. This time they reached back.

"Thank you for your time," Principal Carter said. "And for your good work."

"Thanks," Cam said.

"Uh-huh. Thanks," Jackson added.

They left the office and got a few steps down the hall before Cam threw her arms around Jackson.

"This is great!" she yelled, pulling away.

"Yeah, good news," he said, giving her a feeble pat on the back.

"I just . . . I kind of can't believe it. I really didn't think he would choose our side."

"We were right," Jackson said with a shrug.

"Yeah. We really were, huh?" Cam believed in what they were fighting for, and she was willing to keep pushing for her goals. It was validating that the principal agreed with them.

"Come on," Jackson said. "We both know Vivian is waiting to hear all about it."

At lunch they gave her the play-by-play. Viv let out a *whoop* when Cam told her the news about Lenox and the club.

Later on when the three of them were walking to RoboSub, Jeremy turned a corner and locked eyes with Cam. She froze. Jackson and Viv turned to look.

Jeremy had clearly just come from his meeting with the principal, and he was *not* happy. His face was totally flushed, and when he saw Cam, his hands clenched into fists, and his eyes narrowed. But then for whatever reason, he looked away and went right past them. Maybe because Cam wasn't alone, or because of the look on Viv's face, or maybe he'd finally gotten tired of making Cam's life hard.

"Somebody isn't too happy," Viv said with a wink. "Man, Oprah was right. Success *is* the best revenge."

"We still have RoboSub," Cam reminded her. "And he's still president."

"Maybe so," Viv said. "But you have the administration's attention now, and they're on your side. It's easy to pick on someone you think is small and alone. But you were *never* small, and now he understands that you aren't alone either. Bullies want easy targets. You defeated the boss!"

"Yeah, but I'm not sure he's the big boss," Jackson said.

"What do you mean?" Viv asked.

"Like, this is the Brock gym, but there are a lot more gyms."

Just like my dream, Cam thought.

"The Brock gym?" Viv asked.

Jackson rolled his eyes. "It's a Pokémon thing. Honestly, did you two grow up under a rock?"

They laughed and entered the design lab—Cam and her two best friends.

Jeremy and Matt were talking in hushed tones in the middle of the lab. Normally everyone split up into teams and got to work, but something was clearly going on.

Jeremy gesticulated, speaking fast. As Matt listened, his expression went from concerned to surprised to understanding.

"Think it's something with San Diego?" Jeff asked the electrical group.

"Nah. We're all registered," Liam said. "I confirmed our team stuff."

"Maybe a rule change or something. Or a new task?" Greg wondered.

But Cam knew what it was. Matt and Jeremy faced the room.

"We have some news to share," Matt said, glancing at Jeremy.

"Yeah. Mr. Lenox will no longer be advising this club," Jeremy said.

Silence. Mr. Lenox hadn't been a presence anyway.

Spencer spoke first. "Okay. So who's our faculty advisor now?"

Before Jeremy could respond, someone came in carrying a box so large only two feet in clogs were visible.

I recognize those shoes, Cam thought.

"Greetings, RoboSub team!" Ms. Newberry said, putting the box on a workstation. "Oh, I'm so sorry. Did I interrupt? I'm Ms. Newberry. Are you the copresidents?"

Jeremy scowled. Matt recovered fast.

"Hey, I'm Matt," he said, shaking Ms. Newberry's hand. "And this is Jeremy."

"Well, don't let me interrupt your work! I want to let you all know I'll advise the club for the rest of the year. And I'll find a second chaperone to join us in San Diego."

The rest of the room still seemed stunned.

"Ms. N, what's in the box?" Viv asked.

"Ah!" Ms. Newberry started pulling things out. "I grabbed some things I had in the studio." Out came several glass bottles. "In case anyone was interested in experimenting." A big ball of wrapped clay. "Or looking for some inspiration!"

Is that a xylophone? Cam asked silently.

"So, wait. Will you be our advisor next year too?" Jeff asked.

"Oh, no. I'm already spoken for," Ms. Newberry said, with a sly look at Cam. "But I'm unattached this year and happy to help."

"All right. So . . . let's get to work," Jeremy said.

Half an hour later, Jeremy called Matt and the leads over to his workstation.

Viv and Cam shared a look, then Viv darted over.

"What do you think they're talking about?" she asked.

"Who knows," Cam said. They were partially obscured behind a rolling shelf full of electronics, so they could see without obviously watching.

Jeremy's body language was agitated. Matt and Liam were facing Cam. Matt was annoyed with whatever Jeremy was saying, and Liam's face grew skeptical. Matt tried to cut in a few times, but Jeremy just kept talking.

Then Liam erupted. "No! We're not doing that," he said, loud enough for the whole room to hear. "Is this meeting over? I have work to do." He left the group without waiting for a response.

"Oh shit!" Viv said, diving around the corner of the shelf so Liam wouldn't see her.

Liam sat back down and looked at the board he'd been working on. Cam tried not to notice him, but the curiosity was killing her.

Liam looked up and Cam snapped her head down, pretending she hadn't been looking at him moments before.

"Hey, Cam?"

"Mm-hmm?" She tried to be casual.

"I just want you to know I think you do great work. I'm glad you're on the electrical team, and I hope you'll be on it next year. Honestly . . . you might be a good person to lead it."

Viv gasped from behind the shelf.

"Oh . . . um . . . thanks. I mean, you don't think Jeff should do it?"

"No, I don't," he said. "I think you work hard and know your stuff." He leaned in closer, and his voice softened. They were sitting at the same workstation, and when he leaned in, his elbow brushed hers, but he didn't move it.

"I've noticed you during meetings. I mean—" *Was he blushing?* "I mean, like, I've noticed how you act. Because it can be hard, and it's just you and Viv."

"Uh-huh," Cam said. All she could think about was the point where their elbows were still touching.

"I hope you'll both stick with it," he said with a smile. "And I'm putting your name forward for team lead next year."

Leading the electrical team? She hadn't considered that, but it could be cool.

Why not me? she wondered.

He glanced away, his demeanor changing. "Um, and I was also thinking. Well, I guess I was wondering—"

"Hey," Matt said, joining them at the table.

Liam snapped back like he'd been electrocuted where their elbows made contact. Behind the electrical cabinet, Viv failed to stifle an *ugh*. Cam coughed to cover it.

"Such bullshit," Matt said, looking at Liam. "I'm so done with him."

Liam nodded. "I mean, what the hell?"

"Um, can someone clue me in?" Cam asked.

Matt sat down. "He said if Ms. Newberry can't find another chaperone, we'll go to San Diego with only ten members, so you and Viv would stay behind."

This again?

"Which is total bullshit, because we literally need Viv to do the presentation," Matt went on.

"And you two aren't the only sophomores. What about Jackson? Shouldn't we draw straws or something?" Liam said.

"It's not even an issue," Matt said. "Like, Ms. Newberry said she'd get another chaperone."

"Why is he allowed to pick who stays behind?" Cam asked.

"He isn't," Matt said. "I'm the copresident, and I'm vetoing. Like, enough, dude."

"Kinda wild about Lenox, huh?" Liam asked. "Can't say I'll miss him. He wasn't ever here anyway."

"Right?" Matt said.

Cam's ears burned. *Do they know he's gone because of me?*

"I don't know what's goin' on. Jeremy stormed in and said Lenox was out, Newberry was in, and we had to announce it." Matt shrugged. "Anyway, let me know if either of you hear anything else about San Diego, okay?"

There was suddenly a crash behind them. Viv fell from behind the electrical shelf.

"Shit!" she exclaimed, regaining her footing. "Haha. Who put that there? Am I right? So clumsy. Cam, may I have a word?"

Viv grabbed her arm and pulled her into the nearest breakout room.

"Ohmigod, he almost asked you out," Viv gushed.

"Huh?" Cam was still thinking about the San Diego trip and

whether Lenox disappearing would somehow be tied back to her.

"Liam! Hello!"

"Oh," Cam said. "Oh! Ohmigod! Do you think so?"

"Totally," Viv said. "I almost tackled Matt when he interrupted."

"Whoa," Cam said. "I mean... do you think he'll ask again?"

"Time will tell, my friend," Viv said. "Time will tell."

< br >

A month later Mom screamed "Yes!" in the middle of the kitchen, which caused Cam to drop her spoon into her Cheerios.

It's too early for yelling, Cam thought.

"What is it?" Dad asked.

"I just got off the phone with Joe, the firm's owner," Mom said. "They decided to remove Shane from staff. Completely."

"Mom! That's amazing!" Cam said, jumping up to hug her. "I'm so proud of you."

Mom hugged her. "Thank you, nena. I'm proud of myself."

Dad put his arms around them both. "Look at these fierce ladies, kickin' butt and takin' names."

Cam rolled her eyes. "Okay, Dad, cheese factor ten thousand."

They settled back around the counter. "What about Marissa?" Cam asked. "Did you end up telling them about what happened?"

"I didn't need to," Mom said. "When she found out we were reporting Shane for other things, she wanted to share what happened to her. She knew we all supported her. I wasn't about to let them fire her," she said with a wink.

A grin spread across Cam's face. *Pretty cool*, she thought.

"Well, who's going to be the new manager?" Dad asked.

"We'll see," Mom said, sipping her coffee. "But I'll definitely apply again."

Cam's phone pinged. It was a text from Viv. **Study sesh?**

"Gotta go," Cam said, drinking the rest of the milk from her bowl. "Studying with Viv."

Finals were coming up, and now that her CS project and Viv's DECA competition were done, they had only a few weeks to cram before the end of the year. Then the RoboSub team would move the sub and parts to Matt's garage so they could keep working until the competition in July. Only one month away.

```
(function imposter(){
    console.log("Chapter");
    console.log("Nineteen");
})();
```

Chapter Nineteen

One morning in July, Cam woke to the sound of honking outside. Glancing at her clock, she shot up in bed. She had overslept.

Rushing to the window, she saw Viv leaning in her car window to honk the horn again. "Are you alive?" she shouted when she saw Cam. "I texted and called!"

Underneath Cam, the front door opened and she heard her mother's voice. "Ay. You'll wake the whole neighborhood, Vivian. Come inside and have something to eat."

Viv looked up at Cam and pointed to an imaginary watch.

"I get it, I get it," Cam mumbled to herself, stumbling to the shower.

Thirty minutes later, after she had torn through the bathroom and thrown on jeans and a T-shirt, she grabbed her suitcase. *Thank god I packed last night*, she thought as she headed downstairs. Viv was sipping a coffee with Cam's parents in the kitchen.

"There she is!" Cam's dad said. "I made you a breakfast burrito for the road."

"Great. Thanks!" she said, taking a bite while she threw on a light jacket.

"Slept through your alarm, huh?" Viv asked.

Cam mumbled "Yeah" around her burrito.

Viv looked at the clock above the stove. "Well, the good news is I'm early because I'm excited, so we're now right on time! Thanks for the coffee, Goldbergs. Always a pleasure."

Cam's mom came around the island to give Cam a hug. "My baby is going across the country without me!" she said. "Be careful, nena."

"Yeah. Don't do anything you wouldn't do if we were there," her dad said, also coming in for a hug. "I mean, standing *right there*."

Cam rolled her eyes. "Yeah, yeah. I get it. Be good, don't do drugs, etcetera, etcetera."

"Okay, let's hit it!" Viv said, grabbing Cam's bag.

"San Diego, here we come!" Cam said, giddy with excitement. California. Without her parents. With her best friend. With Liam.

< br >

The RoboSub team piled into the school bus, stacking suitcases in the back. They were using one of the smaller buses that the sports teams took to away games. Ms. Newberry was driving, and Mr. Winston would meet them at the airport. The physics teacher had volunteered to be the other chaperone.

Ms. Newberry's presence at RoboSub had changed the vibe completely over the last two months. Gone were the power moves and microaggressions that Jeremy had lorded over them. He was far from friendly, but he'd cleaned up his act some.

Viv and Cam took a seat together near the front of the bus. When Liam got on, he gave Cam an extra-long smile, and she tried not to blush. They'd worked closely, getting the sub ready for competition, but he still hadn't asked her out.

Before school ended, Principal Carter kept his word. Cam had two meetings with him and other members of the administration to talk about her experiences in class, the vibe around school when it came to things like CS and RoboSub, and the data she uncovered through her research. They looked concerned, took a lot of notes, and asked if they could meet with her again the next year.

And now it was time for San Diego.

The team didn't expect to win or even do very well. If they could get past the qualifying round, that would be more than any high-school team had managed the year before. Cam felt confident they could do it.

This trip was also the farthest Cam had ever been from home, and the only time traveling without her parents. The ratio of kids to adults made everything feel more exciting. The long bus ride to the airport meant more time to hang with Viv and whisper about Liam. Another hour wait to board the plane. Liam sat in the row of chairs facing Cam and Viv, and every once in a while he looked up at her and smiled.

< br >

The San Diego airport was crowded, bright, and disorienting. They learned the hard way about Southern California traffic, and after what felt like an entire day, they finally pulled up to the hotel.

It reminded Cam of apartment complexes on TV shows—a big U-shaped hotel with a pool in the middle and the rooms accessed from outside. The hotel manager had agreed that starting at nine each night, the team could use the pool to test the sub and troubleshoot.

The team all had rooms facing the courtyard with the pool.

"The better to see you with, my dears," Viv said with an eyebrow wriggle.

Ms. Newberry had given them a speech on the way from the airport, and the rules were simple.

- School rules still apply, so don't break them.
- Don't be where you aren't supposed to be, ever.
- Do be where you *are* supposed to be, at all times.
- If you break a rule, you're heading home. Immediately. School would follow up with additional consequences.

Her tone made it clear that she was not messing around. Cam definitely didn't want to get in trouble, and she *really* didn't want to get sent home, so she planned to be exactly where she was supposed to be all the time. Cam and Viv's room was right next to Ms. Newberry's, so if someone so much as came by to talk to them, she would know.

Viv nudged Cam and pointed out that Liam's room was opposite theirs. He gave them a wave and disappeared inside.

"Ohmigod. You could, like, put notes in the window for him. So cute," Viv said.

Cam laughed. "I don't think we're there yet."

"But you could get there on this trip!"

The room was simple: two beds, a bathroom, a TV, a dresser, and a small desk. They dropped their bags and plopped down on the beds. Ms. Newberry had given them the afternoon to rest after the long flight. They had a late night ahead, and only two days to test before their qualifying round at the Transducer Evaluation Center.

< br >

The team was in trouble. Matt was in the water with the sub, and everyone else was scattered around the edge of the pool with tools and laptops. The sub submerged and resurfaced without a problem, but when they tried to move it forward twenty feet and spin, the sub went forward, bumped the wall of the pool, and froze. Matt had to dive down and grab it. Three times now.

"It's gotta be a code problem," Matt said, bringing the sub back to start over.

"It's not a code problem!" Jeremy almost shouted.

Ms. Newberry looked over at them from her lounge chair.

Jeremy lowered his voice. "The propeller is getting stuck. The code tells it to rotate right here." He pointed to his laptop screen. "So it must be the hardware."

"The propeller is fine," Spencer said. He'd removed the motor component and plugged it into his laptop. When he hit a key, the propeller whirred to life without an issue.

"Well, then, maybe it's the connection," Matt suggested. "Last year we had issues with redundancy."

Liam shook his head. "Airtight connection. We fixed those issues from last year. Cam cleaned that all up." He gave her a nod and she tried not to blush.

Then she had an idea.

"Does it run underwater on its own?" she asked.

"What do you mean?" Spencer said.

"You know—the motor by itself. Did we account for the weight of the water?"

The boys looked at each other. Spencer shrugged. He handed Matt the propeller. Matt put it underwater and Spencer ran the code again. The motor sputtered a bit, but it wouldn't run.

Matt smiled. "That's gotta be it! Great work, Cam."

She smiled as some of the other boys echoed Matt's praise. Jackson started to fix the code to run the motor with increased resistance. Jeremy glared but said nothing.

"That was amazing!" Viv said later on in their room. "You, like, totally saved the team."

Cam shrugged. "Thanks. It was pretty cool, right?"

"*So* cool," Viv replied. "And the look on Jeremy's face. Truly priceless."

Their first day on the TRANSDEC was tomorrow, and Cam was nervous. She desperately wanted to qualify so they could participate in at least one official round. It would be so disappointing to come all this way just to turn around and go back home. Neither girl could sleep.

"What are you most excited for?" Viv asked.

"To meet other teams, I think," Cam said. "They're from all over the world, and a lot of colleges are here."

"You're always thinking about college," Viv said with a sigh. "Once we're actually there, what will you spend all your time worrying about?"

"Well, grad school, probably," Cam replied, and they both laughed.

```
(function imposter(){
    console.log("Chapter");
    console.log("Twenty");
})();
```

Chapter Twenty

Competition day one. They piled onto the bus with gear and the sub. Cam was so nervous she couldn't eat breakfast. Her stomach grumbled as they unloaded in the parking lot.

Registration went pretty fast, and they each got a lanyard with their school and name on it. Little tents were set up all around the TRANSDEC. They found their tent and started unpacking. Once they were settled, Ms. Newberry told them they had a few hours until their trial run and gave them permission to walk around.

Cam and Viv wandered and scoped out the other subs. Cam kept trying to remember to call them AUVs—after all, autonomous underwater vehicle was the actual term. It was fun to see how different teams had added flavor with color and design choices. To Cam's disappointment (though she wasn't surprised), most of the teams were either all boys or had just one or two women. Cam and Viv were about to head back to their tent when a bunch of laughter caught Cam's attention. She looked over at a group of young women hard at work.

Approaching their tent, Cam heard Adele playing softly. One of the girls looked up and caught Cam's eye.

"Hi!" the girl said. "Come on over."

Cam tugged Viv's arm.

"Hey, I'm Mallory." A girl with a messy top bun and a Robo-Sub sticker on her laptop stood up to shake hands. Cam and Viv introduced themselves.

"What team are you from?" Mallory asked.

"We're here from MacArthur High School in Ohio," Viv replied.

"A high-school team! Cool! We all go to Texas A&M."

"I didn't think that was a women's college," Cam said.

Mallory laughed. "Nope. We have an all-female team, but the university is coed."

"They let you do that?" Viv asked, giving Cam a little nudge.

"Oh, totally," Mallory said. "Here. Take this. We have a website and everything." She gave them each a sticker with QR codes. "We have a Women in Engineering program," Mallory went on. "Are either of you interested in engineering?"

"Cam is," Viv said. "And she's obsessed with what college she should go to."

Cam blushed a little. "Yeah. I'm maybe interested."

"That's great!" Mallory said. "You should look for schools that highlight women in engineering in marketing and on the website. There are a lot of engineering programs that sort of ignore women, but being in a space where you can get resources is really helpful."

After the school year she'd had, it was hard for Cam to believe such a thing could even exist.

"Here, take my number," Mallory said. Cam pulled out her phone and added it. "Text me if you have questions."

"I will!" Cam said.

"Good luck out there," Mallory said. "We're here if you need anything. Everybody likes to help each other at these competitions."

"That's great! Thanks so much!" Viv said. "Um, that was pretty amazing."

"Yeah. I didn't even realize a girls' team was an option." Cam's head was spinning.

"I wonder if any students there complained about being excluded," Viv said, rolling her eyes.

"I doubt those girls care," Cam said. Mallory's words gave her a lot to think about. Cam was doing some research on colleges with engineering programs, but it hadn't occurred to her to look for programs specifically for women, or programs with resources for women in engineering and STEM.

Back at their own tent, people were fiddling with the sub. There was nervous energy in the air. To get into the semifinal round, their sub needed to autonomously pass through the underwater gate during a practice run. The first was today, and they'd have another chance tomorrow. The TRANSDEC was much larger than anything they practiced in up till this point.

An hour later, their team was called. Only Jeremy and Matt represented them. Cam went to the sidelines with the rest of the team, where they could see close-up footage on the jumbotron. They had twenty minutes total of practice time, and the first five were for prep. Cam watched the guys fidget. They were clearly nervous.

Five minutes passed. The end of prep.

Because the pool was so large and deep, no team member went in. Subs were lowered into the water by a little crane. Jeremy leaned over to adjust a few final things before leaning back and signaling to the officials that they were ready. An official was in the water with snorkel gear to follow the sub's path. He would also recover the sub if it strayed off task and bring it back for another run, if they chose to do one.

Cam held her breath and watched the screen as their sub disappeared underwater. It made a beeline for the gate. So far, so good. But about halfway there, the sub stopped. Cam hoped it was some sort of glitch, but the AUV began to spin. It performed three tight circles—something they had programmed it to do later—and stopped again, suspended in the water. The official collected it and swam back to the deck where Jeremy and Matt waited.

Jeremy typed furiously on his laptop. He signaled to the official to run it again. They were allowed as many runs as time permitted, and so far they had used only four of their fifteen minutes.

The second run began like the first. The sub went under and headed right for the gate. It went farther this time, and Viv clutched Cam's arm in excitement. About ten feet from the gate, however, it stopped, spun around three times, and hung suspended in the water.

Liam put his hands over his face and groaned, then crossed his arms. "What's the problem?" he asked no one in particular.

The official brought the sub back. This time Jeremy and Matt argued about something. Only seven minutes left. Enough time for one more run.

Cam could tell Jeremy was angry—she could almost hear him shouting. Matt fiddled with the sub, then signaled. The same thing happened on the third run. Deflated, Cam watched as the AUV was removed from the water. Tomorrow they'd have another chance, but they needed to figure out what was wrong. Jeremy still looked furious.

"Well, my turn next," Viv said. Her design presentation was in thirty minutes. She would present her work to a panel of judges.

They made their way to the presentation area. Cam found a seat with a good view. Someone took the empty seat on her right.

"Hey," Jackson said.

"Oh, hey!" Cam replied. "I didn't realize you had time to come to this."

"Vivian's my friend," he said.

Cam smiled. He wasn't wrong. "I'm sure she'll really appreciate the support," Cam said.

"She doesn't need it. She'll do a great job."

They sat through three presentations before it was Viv's turn. From the looks on the judges' faces, they felt as bored as the audience. The reports were dry, and presenters spoke mostly in monotones, reading numbers that didn't connect to anything off a page.

When Viv took the stage, she approached each judge and shook their hand. This seemed to perk them up as they readjusted in their seats to accommodate her polite gesture. This was DECA training at work. Cam had never seen Viv compete before, and she swelled with how impressed she was.

Viv told a story—a recap of the last few months of work and the cast of characters along the way. All the business data was there, and Viv had the information to back it up. But she didn't just read her report—she performed. The audience laughed with her, and all three judges smiled broadly when she finished and thanked them. She left the stage to loud applause.

"Viv, that was incredible!" Cam said afterward.

"Yeah? Do you think we'll get full points?" Viv asked.

"I know we will!" Cam replied.

"Great job, Vivian," Jackson said, smiling at her.

"Thanks," Viv said.

Did Cam detect a slight blush? *No, it can't be*, Cam thought. Viv was too level-headed, and she'd never blush about Jackson. *Right?*

< br >

After a totally stressful dinner, the team all put on their swimsuits and headed to the pool to troubleshoot. Viv came down for moral support and posted up with a magazine on a lounge chair.

"The code is right, so I don't even wanna hear anybody say that's the problem," Jeremy said.

"Well, there was no electrical damage, so it's also not electrical," Liam countered.

"Listen, it's gotta be something," Matt said, trying to keep the peace. "And it's not a big deal, we just need to figure it out and fix it."

After several adjustments they practiced making the sub go much deeper to pass through an imaginary gate, and it seemed to be working.

"It worked yesterday too," Spencer pointed out. "And then we ate it on the TRANSDEC."

Everybody looked at him. He shrugged. "It's the truth."

"Well, what about the size difference?" Viv said from her perch, turning a page.

They all turned in her direction.

"What did you say?" Jeremy asked.

"You know," Viv said, still engrossed in her reading. "Adjust for the size of the TRANSDEC. It was, like, huge. Did you put that in your calculations or whatever? Like Cam said yesterday about the water, but, you know, more?"

They were silent.

Viv looked up. "What? Is that dumb?"

"No," Matt said, smiling broadly. "That might be the smartest thing anyone's said all night."

They pulled out notebooks and looked up stats about the TRANSDEC. The environment was different from where they'd tested, so of course they didn't know conclusively what would happen in the TRANSDEC. They made some adjustments, updated the code, and went back to their rooms with their fingers crossed.

"Wow! You're really the VIP of this trip," Cam said as they sprawled on their beds, flipping through TV channels.

"Can't help it. I gotta be awesome wherever I go, you know?" Viv said with a wink. "Hey," she continued, getting up from the bed. "I'm gonna get more ice. I'm craving an ice-cold beverage."

Cam continued searching for something to watch. A few seconds later, she realized Viv had forgotten to take the ice bucket, so she grabbed it and her room key and made her way to the stairwell. She was midway down the stairs when she saw Viv and Jackson at the ice machine. She was about to call out to them when she noticed Viv's body language. Jackson glanced up, and on instinct Cam crouched down, clutching the ice bucket, the staircase railing obscuring her from view. Luckily, Jackson turned back to Viv. And Cam realized she could hear them and mostly see them too.

". . . the semifinals," Viv said.

"Yeah, we'll see," Jackson responded, hands in his pockets. "I didn't really expect to win or anything with all these colleges here and stuff."

"Totally," Viv replied.

Cam could only see the side of Viv's face, but was that . . . her moony face? Did Viv *like* Jackson?

No, Cam thought. *I'm imagining this*. Still, she craned her neck and kept listening.

"Your business presentation was really good today," Jackson said.

"You think so?" Viv asked.

Did Viv just do a little hair flip? Move a bit closer?

"Yeah, I don't understand any of that stuff," Jackson said.

"Well, I don't understand any of the stuff you do, so . . ."

They both laughed a little.

"I think you do a good job explaining it to people. When my sister talks about work stuff, I just tune out. I have no idea what she's talking about. But when you talk about that stuff, I get it more, you know?"

"That's really sweet of you," Viv replied.

This time she *definitely* took a step closer. Jackson seemed oblivious that she was close enough to . . .

Jackson shrugged, "Yeah, well, I—"

Viv leaned in. *Was she going to kiss him?* Cam gasped and clamped a hand over her mouth, hoping they didn't hear.

Jackson dodged backward like an athlete. His feet were still planted, but his face was as far from Viv's as possible.

"Whoa, Vivian. Um . . ."

Viv gave a little laugh. "It's okay. That was sort of unannounced."

Cam could tell from her voice that Viv still thought the kiss might happen, as if Jackson just needed to process first.

"Um, I don't . . ." He took a step back.

"I know it feels random," Viv said.

Cam cringed. Her best friend was missing all the cues, and there was nothing she could do.

"No, it's not that—" Jackson started, but Viv didn't let him finish.

"But it's actually not that random, because I'm PrezRoslin."

Jackson froze in place. "What?"

"You know, from *HotS*. PrezRoslin. She's me. Or I'm her. Or whatever."

Jackson's expression was new to Cam. Finally he furrowed his brow and said, "So you've been talking to me online and playing *HotS* all this time?"

"Yeah!" Viv said, like it was no big deal.

I knew it wasn't a good idea, Cam thought.

"Why didn't you tell me it was you?" Jackson looked more confused than angry.

"Oh, um. I don't know." Viv looked down and shuffled her feet. "I guess once we played a little and I didn't tell you it was me, it felt weird to tell you later. So I just, like . . . didn't tell you. But it's totally me! And all the conversations we had, those were me too."

Jackson ran a hand through his hair like he was thinking.

"Yeah, so. Surprise!" Viv said. "Maybe now we can, you know, hang out in real life." As she said this, she closed the space between them again.

"Viv. Whoa. I mean, this is really flattering, it's just that . . ."

Uh oh, Cam thought. *Viv is about to get fully rejected.*

". . . I have a girlfriend," Jackson finished.

Cam's jaw dropped.

Viv's jaw dropped.

"You what?"

"Uh, yeah. We've been together for, like, six months now," Jackson said.

"Who is she?" Viv said, her curiosity clearly overriding any humiliation.

"We met online playing *HotS*. She, um . . . lives in Indiana. Anyway, yeah. I don't want to, like, give you the wrong idea or anything. I do have a girlfriend."

Cam couldn't tell who was more uncomfortable. Jackson for turning down a girl for what Cam was pretty sure was the first time in his life, or Vivian who probably thought Jackson would be ecstatic to learn that a cute girl liked him and was playing his favorite game all this time.

"Oh," Viv said. Her voice sounded small now.

"I'm really sorry if I did anything to, you know, give you the wrong impression or whatever," Jackson said.

Viv took a step back, put a hand to her head, and turned to

go. "No! No, you're fine," she said. "I, um. Sorry. I need to go." She turned to walk away.

"Viv?" Jackson called after her.

She put up a hand and kept walking. "Nope. I'm good. Just need to go away from here."

Cam was so busy watching the action, she forgot Viv would come right past her. Cam's limbs shot out in a clumsy mess as she started to get up. The ice bucket exploded out of her lap, and she collapsed down on the stairs in front of Viv. Her friend smirked at the performance, then looked over at the ice machine and realized Cam had witnessed everything.

Viv sighed and joined Cam on the steps, putting her head in her hands. "You saw all that."

"Yep."

"You heard all that?"

"Yep."

"So, that was real. That was a real thing I just did?"

"Oh yeah. Yep. Definitely."

Viv groaned. "This is a literal nightmare."

"I mean, I won't lie, no one's more surprised about what just happened than me. Except, you know, maybe Jackson."

Viv groaned again.

"But at least it was relatively private. And now you don't have to tell me about it! And you *know* Jackson's not gonna say anything to anybody."

"Except his girlfriend!" Viv nearly shouted.

"Right, except his girlfriend. Because, you know. He has a girlfriend, apparently." Cam shifted a little and put an arm around Viv. "Which really, in the scope of things, is the twist of the century, huh?"

Viv hung her head and laughed. "I don't know why I assumed he would just be, like, excited that a girl wanted to be with him. That was so freakin' rude!"

Cam just nodded. Viv wasn't wrong.

"Like, obviously it's shocking that he has a girlfriend, because he never mentioned it. But why *would* he mention it, right?"

"Right," Cam said.

"I'm such a fool," Viv replied.

"Nah, don't say that."

"It's true," Viv said, sniffling a little.

There was a pause, and the sniffling stopped. Cam asked the question she really wanted an answer to.

"So you like Jackson, or . . ."

"I feel crazy."

"It's not crazy if you like Jackson! You just never mentioned it. You know, in the five hundred conversations we have every day."

"I know," Viv said, looking up. "I think I was embarrassed."

"Why?" Cam asked.

"I don't know. I think . . . if I'm honest, I think I made a lot of assumptions about Jackson, a lot of them probably not fair. And I guess he's just not, like, my type? You know what I mean?"

"Yeah," Cam said. "I know what you mean." And she did. Jackson was a Magic-playing, online-gaming, semi–social outcast. He wasn't exactly the center of conversation when it came to potential partners. That wasn't fair, really, but it was true.

Viv sighed. "Anyway, I told him I catfished him. And then tried to make out with him like the world's biggest asshole. So now he'll probably never want to talk to me again. Sorry if that makes things weird with the two of you."

"I bet it won't," Cam said, and she meant it. Jackson was a very reasonable person. The catfishing was not cool, that was for sure. But Cam doubted very much that Jackson would be weird to Viv for the rest of their lives because she tried to kiss him on the RoboSub trip.

"I, on the other hand, have lots of additional questions," Cam said with a wry smile.

Viv put out her hands. "Nope. I'm using the card. We must never speak of this."

"But—"

"I'm playing it!" Viv said, waving an imaginary card in the air. "We never speak of it."

"Oh, fine," Cam said, crossing her arms. "That's no fun, but have it your way."

"Can we go back to the room?" Viv asked.

"Well, we really do need some ice," Cam said.

"Fine, get it." Viv got halfway up the staircase and turned back to Cam. "I mean it!" she shouted. "We must never speak of it!"

Cam laughed. "Okay, okay. I hear you!" She made a zipper motion with her hand across her mouth and pretended to throw away the key.

```
(function imposter(){
    console.log("Chapter");
    console.log("Twenty-One");
})();
```

Chapter Twenty-One

The next morning they piled into the bus and went to the TRANSDEC. They needed to double-check everything before their second qualifying run. This was their only shot at advancing into the semifinals.

Viv took the window seat to avoid Jackson. "I'm going to talk to him," she assured Cam. "I just need to be in my feelings for a minute."

When they got to the tent, everyone started running tests. Vivian's score wouldn't be released unless they qualified for the semifinals. The qualifying runs weren't scored, so points didn't matter yet. Everyone was stressed. An official came to tell the team it was time.

Matt and Jeremy looked tense as they approached the TRANSDEC. Everyone watched as the crane lowered the sub into the pool. When the timer started at fifteen minutes, Jeremy initiated the sub. Like the day before, it went straight for the gate. A good sign.

Was it slowing down as it got deeper? Cam couldn't tell.

Now the sub was thirty feet from the gate.

Twenty feet.

Viv clutched Cam's arm. They both held their breath.

Ten feet.

The sub sputtered a little and it seemed like it might stop. The girls gasped. Then, like the Little Engine That Could, it proceeded through the gate and onward. The team cheered from across the TRANSDEC, and Cam was sure the viewing deck was cheering too.

They had done it. They were going to the next round.

< br >

That night at dinner most of the team was excited to work on the sub more.

"Why bother?" Jeremy said. "We're not going to win."

"But shouldn't we try?" Viv asked. "It's, like, a learning experience."

Jeremy just shrugged and got up for seconds.

Matt responded instead. "We never expect to win this thing. The top college engineering programs in the world are here. We don't have enough resources, enough manpower—sorry, enough peoplepower—or the content knowledge. There's just no way we'd ever even place. Maybe if there was a high-school division, we'd have a shot."

"Do you think they'll ever add one?" Cam asked.

Matt shrugged. "Don't know. Maybe if there were more interest?" He took a bite of his burger. "Anyway, this is a big victory. We should celebrate!"

After a few practice runs in the pool, they all went to their rooms. A few minutes later, Cam and Viv both got a text from a number they didn't know.

Game room. 20 minutes. Don't narc.

"Ohmigod, a secret field-trip party!" Viv said, jumping to her feet.

"We can't go," Cam said.

"Um, no. We have to go," Viv countered. She was already digging through her clothes. "We will not be the nerds who watched *Law & Order* on cable during a secret party."

"Ms. Newberry will know!" Cam said. The rules were very clear, and Cam was not about to get sent home.

"Ms. Newberry is asleep," Viv replied, pulling out a dress and tossing it on the bed. "And we'll be quiet. We'll turn out the lights. Look, we can even leave the blinds open a bit and put pillows in our beds so it looks like we're in here."

That felt really sneaky to Cam. Which probably meant it was bad.

"Come on," Viv pressed, seeing the look on Cam's face. "This could be your last chance to connect with Liam!"

Viv had a point. There hadn't been much opportunity for Cam to talk to Liam since they'd left Ohio, and the window was closing. He was going away to work at a camp in August, and she wouldn't see him until school started. This might be her last chance.

"Fine. But I want to stay for only like a half hour," Cam said, getting up and considering the clothes Viv had pulled out for her.

"I'll take it," Viv said with a grin.

< br >

The girls opened and closed their door as softly as possible and scurried to the stairwell. It was quiet outside. They were in the clear.

As they approached the game room, Cam heard music. She wondered how their classmates had gotten into this room after hours. When they entered it was dark and loud, kind of what

Cam expected of a high-school party. Not that she'd ever been to one. There were some arcade games and a pool table. Some of the guys were around the *Pac-Man* machine.

"There's Liam," Viv said. "I'll be back."

Liam was leaning against a wall watching other guys play pool. Cam spotted Jackson, who was gaming on his laptop in the corner. Trying not to think too hard about it, Cam approached Liam.

"Hey, Liam!" she said. *Too perky. Definitely too perky*, she thought.

"Hey, Cam. I'm glad you came," he replied, putting his hand out a little. She took it as a signal to join him and leaned on the wall. "Big day today."

"Yeah. It was exciting!" Cam exclaimed. *Relax. Geez!*

"Yeah. It's awesome to make it to the scored round," Liam said. "Even if we can't place. Definitely further than last year."

"Totally. Yeah." *Wow. Insightful, Cam.*

"So are you excited for next year?"

She shrugged. "Not as excited as you probably are. You know, with college applications."

He laughed and looked off thoughtfully. "I don't know. I'm ready to start that, but it's also kinda sad to think about leaving high school. Nothing will be the same after, you know? And it's going to be so much work. I'm planning to step down as electrical lead so I can focus on my applications."

"Totally," she said, though she couldn't imagine that yet. "You won't even participate in RoboSub?"

"I don't think so. You know, it'll be hard to leave behind so many cool people," he said, looking at her.

Was he talking about her? It definitely seemed like he was talking about her. He was smiling right at her.

"I think it's really cool that you joined RoboSub this year," he went on. Did he lean a little closer or did she? "You added a lot to the team. And I heard about your club next year. That's a great idea."

"Um, thanks," she said. *Don't look at his mouth. Don't look at his mouth.*

"I hope you'll consider being electrical lead," he said. He was definitely leaning closer.

"Me too."

"I really admire how you stand up for people. I think you're brave."

Cam felt like the air was sucked out of her. She leaned toward him, letting her eyes close gently. Finally her fist kiss, and then her first boyfriend. A senior boyfriend.

A hand on her shoulder made her eyes snap back open.

"Uh, Cam. I don't . . . I'm sorry," Liam said. He held her in place, leaning away from her.

Her eyes got wide. Her thoughts raced. *Oh no. Oh god!*

"Cam, I didn't mean to give you the wrong idea." He ran a hand through his hair, clearly uncomfortable. "I think you're really great. That's all I was trying to say."

Cam felt herself nodding mechanically. *Don't puke. Do not puke*, she willed herself.

"So, I'll see you tomorrow?" Liam asked. He sort of nudged her shoulder.

"There you are!" Viv's voice rang through Cam's haze. "I've been looking everywhere for this gal," Viv said to Liam, putting an arm around Cam. "Come on, I've got something to tell you."

Before Cam knew it, she was pulled through the party and outside.

"Tell me," Viv said.

"What? You said *you* have something to tell *me*," Cam replied.

"That was obviously a lie to get you out of there!" Viv said.

Cam suddenly realized Viv had seen the whole thing. "I can't believe I did that," she said. "Did I just do that?"

Viv nodded with sympathy. "If by *that* you mean *do a total lean in and get stopped with eyes closed and lips puckered*, then yes, you did."

"Ohmigod," Cam said, burying her face in her hands.

"It's okay," Viv said, wrapping her in a hug. "I guess it's a double-strikeout week for us."

Cam laughed through her tears. "He said how cool and smart and brave I am."

"Oh boy," Viv said.

"And I felt like he was getting really close to me. Was he getting close to me?"

"It was hard to see. But it's loud in there, so maybe that's why he leaned in?"

"Ugh. I felt like I was in a movie moment, you know? Like a kiss moment."

"Totally." Viv rubbed Cam's arm.

"I'm so embarrassed." Cam groaned.

"Nah, don't be. You took a swing. Sometimes we miss."

"Did you talk to Jackson?"

Viv's face got serious. "Yep. I think we're good. I apologized for being a dumb jerk."

Cam laughed. "How did he take it?"

"Oh, very awkwardly," Viv replied. "I think we're both mortified enough to pretend it never happened for as long as we both shall live."

"Does that mean I should do that too?" Cam asked.

"Oh, definitely. He doesn't know that you saw," Viv replied. "Come on. Let's go watch *Law & Order*. I bet we can still catch the big reveal."

```
(function imposter(){
    console.log("Chapter");
    console.log("Twenty-Two");
})();
```

Chapter Twenty-Two

The next morning at breakfast, Ms. Newberry looked stern. Jeremy and two other guys were missing.

"I have an announcement," Ms. Newberry said. "Last night some people decided to sneak out of their rooms and drink."

Viv tried to conceal a gasp, but Cam heard it. They hadn't seen any alcohol last night, but they also hadn't stayed very long. If school rules applied, then that meant...

"The students in question are being escorted to the airport right now and will face disciplinary action back home," Ms. Newberry went on. "We will continue with the competition today as planned. I'm optimistic that the rest of the team can pull together and cover for your peers. Mr. O'Neal, you are now the sole president and our team captain," she said, nodding at Matt.

They finished breakfast silently. Cam was in shock. *People drank on a school trip? So stupid.* Then again, maybe it wasn't surprising, coming from Jeremy.

"Do you think other guys were with them? And didn't get caught somehow?" Viv asked, leaning in to whisper.

"I don't know. How did Ms. Newberry even find out?"

"I heard the night manager found them and kinda freaked out when he saw they were underage," Jackson said, joining them.

"Holy shit. This is so stressful," Viv said.

"I mean, the competition is pretty much over for us anyway," Cam said.

"Cam!" Viv said. "We're in the semifinal!"

Cam's face was blank. Viv looked to Jackson, who also seemed clueless.

"What would you all do without me?" she added with a sigh. "We need speakers. For the interview!"

"Well, I'm sure Matt will go," Cam said.

But she was wrong. When they got to the tent, Matt called a team meeting.

"So look, we gotta do this interview thing. It's not a huge deal. You just introduce the team and the video and then answer the announcer's questions while the sub runs the course. Who wants to do it?"

"Aren't you?" Viv asked.

"No way. I hate that stuff," Matt replied. "That was Jeremy's thing. Besides, Zoz Brooks is one of the announcers. That guy's my hero! *Prototype This* was the bomb. I would totally freeze up. It'd be like that time I ran into Shawn Mendes."

Everyone avoided Matt's gaze. Cam felt Vivian take her hand. She had just enough time to think, *Oh no.*

"We'll do it," Viv said, raising their hands together.

"You will?" Matt asked.

"Sure. Why not? I can speak to the business stuff and the video, and Cam knows her way around the sub like the back of her hand. We can totally handle questions. Besides, we need the rest of you on the deck troubleshooting."

Cam nodded. "Sure. We can do it."

Matt looked at them, then at the team in general. "All right, cool," he said. "Cam and Viv it is. Thanks for helping out."

"Anything for the team," Viv said with a wink.

Cam pulled Viv out of the tent. "What are you doing?"

"Embracing opportunity," she said. "Come on. This'll be great. We're gonna be on TV!"

"It's on YouTube."

"Whatever. Even better!"

"But we don't know what we're talking about," Cam said.

"What? Of course we know what we're talking about! Have we not been here this whole time working on this thing?"

She had a point, but Cam felt nervous. Glancing around, she spotted the announcer's booth to the side of the launch deck. Another team was being interviewed as their sub ran the course. A familiar pit formed in Cam's stomach.

"Hey. It'll be fine," Viv said, putting both hands on Cam's shoulders. "Look at me. We're doing it together!"

Cam took a deep breath. Viv was right—they both knew more than enough to handle the interview. And otherwise they'd just watch from the viewing deck.

"I gotta tell my parents to turn on the YouTube stream," Cam said, whipping out her phone. "They're gonna freak."

"Totally! How's my shirt?" They were both wearing the team T-shirt they'd had on all week.

"Appropriately nerdy," Cam replied with a laugh.

Her parents were typing. Dad's came through first.

Amazing! We're already watching the stream!

Then Mom's.

Nena, wow!!! We can't wait to see you!

About twenty minutes before their team's scheduled run, an official came to take Vivian and Cam to the announcer booth. As they were waiting for their interview, Viv turned to Cam, and asked, "You ready?"

"As ready as I'll ever be," Cam replied.

"Okay. Your turn," an official said, gesturing for them to take the stage.

Two empty chairs were between the two hosts, Zoz Brooks and Tori Mercopolis. The girls took the seats and introduced themselves.

"Are you from an all-girls team?" Tori asked.

"Oh, no," Cam replied. "We just shuffled speakers this morning."

"Cool," Zoz said. "We'll be live in a few minutes. The producer over there will give us a wave when it's time, and another wave when we're done. We won't ask any hardball questions—feel free to share whatever you like."

"We'll introduce the two of you and the team first, and then show your video before commenting on the run," Tori added.

"Excellent," Viv said. "And can I just say, what an honor. I know I speak for my teammates when I say we're big fans of you both."

Zoz and Tori nodded and smiled.

"All right. Ready?" Zoz asked, turning toward the camera.

"Ready," Viv and Cam said.

"Here we are with Cameron Goldberg and Vivian Knix from MacArthur High School in Ohio," Zoz said. "Welcome, Viv and Cam!"

"Hi, Zoz. Hi, Tori," Viv said into her mic.

"Thanks for having us," Cam added.

"So, do you have any comment about your video before we play it for the crowd?" Tori asked.

The girls looked at each other. Cam shrugged.

"I think it speaks for itself," Viv said. "You know, good old high-school fun. We really tried to get creative with the theme."

Honestly, their video wasn't much to write home about. They had struggled to figure out the video without offending anyone who was treated unfairly during the sixties, which was pretty much everyone except white guys. To avoid that, the team decided to go with a focus on technology and how it evolved through the decade.

"Educational," Zoz said with a smile.

"Cam here is our research wizard," Viv said.

"So talk us through your sub process," Tori said, turning to Cam.

It was difficult not to get distracted by what was happening on the deck. The guys brought over the sub, and Matt fiddled with it as it was loaded into the crane. Cam focused on Tori. This was live right now and would stay on YouTube for who knew how long. Starting from the beginning, Cam talked about how the team had formed only last year and grown this year with its first female members. Along the way, she highlighted issues they'd had with the sub, including the snafu with their first run that almost cost them the qualification.

"And here they go on their first run," Zoz mercifully cut in.

They all watched as Tori and Zoz described the sub's run.

"It's cleared the first gate—on to the buoys," Tori said.

"One . . . two . . . oops," Zoz said.

The sub bumped the first and second buoy, but then rose away from the buoys altogether. The diver grabbed it and brought it back to the deck.

"Uh-oh. Got stuck there," Tori said, smiling at Viv.

"You know how it goes, Tori," Viv replied. "I'm glad we get another chance!"

They watched as Matt made some adjustments then relaunched the sub. This time it cleared the gate and hit all three buoys, but then it couldn't find the third task. There wasn't enough time for another run, so Matt waved to the crowd and collected their sub from the official.

"That's a pretty good showing!" Zoz said, wrapping up the interview. "It's always great to see high-school teams here. I hope we'll see you again next year."

"Oh, you will," Viv said. "Quick shout-out to the Goldbergs watching at home!"

Cam and Viv waved at the camera, handed back their mics, and left the podium.

"Um, that was amazing," Viv said. "Finally the fame we deserve!"

Cam laughed. "It was pretty fun."

"And girl, you knew what you were talking about up there. Sometimes you threw around engineering words, and I was like, What is she even talking about? You were impressive!"

"Thanks," Cam said. It was true. She held her own in the interview, and she was kind of an expert on the sub. She'd worked on it a lot, and she'd learned more about engineering and coding than she ever would've guessed. Talking about it with famous engineers on TV (or YouTube, at least) felt pretty validating.

When they got back to the tent, Matt gathered everyone for a team meeting.

"Well, I consider this a win," he said. "We got further than last year, and no matter what our score is, I'm proud of the work we all did."

Everybody clapped.

"But really, let's see what our score is," he added with a grin.

They all huddled together in front of the large scoreboard. There were twenty-five teams total, and the top ten went on to the final round. They didn't expect to advance, but not being last would be a big deal. Just as they started to lose patience and get antsy, their team appeared. In twelfth place.

Cheers erupted all around her, and a huge grin spread across Cam's face. *Twelfth place! Not bad!* Apparently, successfully completing all aspects of the course wasn't that common. An official came by with a score breakdown, and they learned that Viv's design presentation got the highest score of any team.

"Excellent work, everyone!" Ms. Newberry said. "This calls for celebration."

Matt came over and shook Viv's hand. "Hey. Congratulations on that design report. There's no way we would've done so well without you."

Viv did a little hair flip. "Oh, you know, all in a day's work."

"You too, Cam." He turned to her and shook her hand too. "There were so many details you noticed and fixed. I honestly don't think we would've qualified without both of you."

Cam smiled, taking the compliment. "Thanks, Matt. I don't think you would have either."

"Ha! She said it!" Viv said.

Matt laughed the hardest.

```
(function imposter(){
    console.log("Chapter");
    console.log("Twenty-Three");
})();
```

Chapter Twenty-Three

As Cam and Viv pulled into Cam's driveway, Cam's parents waved signs that said "Congratulations RoboSub!" with drawings of the sub and stick figures.

"Ohmigod. Your parents are just the cutest," Viv said.

Mom and Dad cheered when Cam opened her door.

"The return of the victors!" her father exclaimed.

Her mom ran over to give her a hug. "We missed you, nena. We're so proud of you!"

"Thanks, guys. But you know we didn't win, right?"

"To *us* you are winners," her mom countered. "Come, we want to show you your amazing interview."

Cam and Viv hadn't had time to watch after leaving the competition. There was lots of packing back at the hotel, and they'd gone to the airport at six that morning. Cam was exhausted and jetlagged, but she was definitely up for seeing the interview.

They crowded on the couch, and Cam's mom brought over tall glasses of cold milk and cocadas. The video was queued up to their interview, and her father hit play. Cam watched her exchange with Tori and Zoz. It was bizarre—she felt like she was watching someone else. Viv looked like her usual outgoing self, but Cam didn't recognize herself: confident, calm, and smart. Really smart.

She'd had a high-level conversation with two engineers on a livestream. And she noticed something else: the people around her reacting. Viv looked at her with so much admiration, it almost brought tears to Cam's eyes. Tori and Zoz listened as if Cam's words mattered and she knew what she was talking about as a valued member of her team and community. Cam realized that all those things were true.

When the interview ended, her parents hit pause and turned to the girls.

"Crushed it," Viv said, popping a whole cookie into her mouth.

"Wow, I had forgotten a lot of that," Cam said. "It feels like it happened a long time ago."

"I know we've already said this," Cam's dad said, "but we're really proud of you, Cameron. You couldn't have done that a year ago. Think about how far you've come!"

He had a point. Last summer she volunteered at the library and tried to create a new handheld fan that sprayed water and moved air simultaneously. She had no idea about engineering then, and she definitely knew nothing about coding. Now she knew enough of three different languages to program in all three. She worked on an actual robot that could move autonomously underwater. She stood up for girls like her, and girls she hadn't even met yet but would when she launched her new club in the fall. People tried to stop her progress. But she had succeeded anyway.

"We don't care that you didn't win a trophy, nena," her mom said, putting a hand on Cam's knee. "We have seen such change in you. This girl in the interview . . . I am so honored to say she's my daughter."

"Mom, come on. You'll make me cry."

"I mean it," she said, looking into Cam's eyes. "And somewhere out there, younger girls are watching that video and thinking, 'I can do that. Cameron Goldberg did it. Why not me?'"

Cam felt tears run down both cheeks, and Mom encircled her in a tight hug. Within moments, Viv and Dad joined in.

"That's some powerful shit, Mrs. G," Viv said, wiping her eyes. "Pardon my French."

"We'll allow it this once," Cam's dad said with a wink.

After watching more recorded coverage from the competition, Cam walked Viv to her car.

"It's true, you know. What your mom said," Viv said.

"Yeah," Cam said with a sigh. "I think I finally feel that."

"And me too," Viv added. "I know you felt like you dragged me into this, but the opportunity became a big deal. Top presentation score at an international competition? Ivy League, here I come!"

Cam felt herself tearing up again. "Hey, that was all you."

"It was our combined powers," Viv said, pulling Cam into a hug. "I love you, sis."

"I love you too," Cam said.

"All right. Enough of this," Viv said, pulling back and wiping her eyes. "I say we take, like, thirty-six hours off and then get to work on the new club."

"Yeah? You want to help?"

"Of course," Viv replied. "We have to unearth all the little engineering queens who aren't even aware of their powers. How will they find their way to the light without us?"

"Somehow I bet they'd find a way," Cam said.

She meant it. Through all this, the one thing that moved Cam the most was knowing she wasn't alone. Out there—all over the world—there were millions of other girls like her. Girls interested in things that people said they shouldn't care about. Girls pursuing classes and careers and spaces that people said they should have no part in. Girls supporting each other, empowering each other, and encouraging each other to not give up. To just keep trying—one more day and one day at a time.

Finally Cam had joined them. And she was just getting started.

A Note from the Author

I won't lie: I started this book in a rage. I'd been kicking around the tech and education spaces for a while, and I had had it up to here with the misogyny, ageism, and general lack of inclusion I observed and experienced every day. It pissed me off when it happened to me, and it *really* pissed me off when I saw it happening to others.

I was in tears before a meeting one day—a big meeting I worked hard to be invited to, and a bunch of jerks worked hard to make me feel like I shouldn't have been. They were about to win. "I can't go. I can't go sit there with them in that room," I said to my colleagues.

I'll never forget what a good friend said to me. She got very stern, looked me right in the eye, and said, "No. Don't ever leave the room. Have a cry, dry the tears, and go sit in that room. Don't let them make you leave."

She was right. I went to the meeting. I know I'm not the first woman, or honestly even the first non-white-cis-guy, to feel this way working in tech and STEM fields. I know I'm not going to be the last, either.

So here's what I'll say: If you're a man in those spaces, or a person with a voice that is heard and respected, do something. You have power. Your silence is deafening. We need your voices while we build our own.

If you're someone with a passion for tech or STEM and you don't feel welcome: Don't leave the room. Is it harder for you than it is for the folks already in the room? You bet. Should it be that way? Fuck no. Find others who you can lean on for support. Leverage resources to get where you want to go—I've included some here to get you started.

Know that you are intelligent, capable, and worthy. When you get through the door, hold it open for those behind you. Pull more seats around the table. Get in the room, and don't you leave it.

Be the change.

Sources for Direct Quotations

p. 10: Thompson, Clive. "The Secret History of Women in Coding: Computer Programming Once Had Much Better Gender Balance Than It Does Today. What Went Wrong?" *The New York Times Magazine*, February 13, 2009.

p. 43: "Mission." The Processing Foundation, www.processingfoundation.org.

p. 50: "What We Do." Girls Who Code, www.girlswhocode.com.

p. 50: "Girls Who Code Girls, Code Your Own Character Now." Girls Who Code, www.girlswhocodegirls.com.

p. 51: "Code Your Own Universe." Girls Who Code, www.girlswhocodegirls.com.

pp. 80–82: Saujani, Reshma. "Teach Girls Bravery, Not Perfection." TED Talks, 2016. https://www.ted.com/talks/reshma_saujani_teach_girls_bravery_not_perfection?language=en.

Resources

To Learn More About Code and Robotics
Girls Who Code: girlswhocode.com
RoboNation: robonation.org
Processing Foundation: processingfoundation.org
Raspberry Pi Foundation: raspberrypi.org
Adafruit: learn.adafruit.com
Kode with Klossy: kodewithklossy.com
Scratch: scratch.mit.edu
TechGirlz: techgirlz.org
Google's CS First: csfirst.withgoogle.com
Microsoft MakeCode: microsoft.com/en-us/makecode
MIT App Inventor: appinventor.mit.edu
Code.org: code.org
freeCodeCamp: freecodecamp.org
Hour of Code: hourofcode.com

For Information About Women in STEM Fields
National Girls Collaborative Project: ngcproject.org
Code First Girls: codefirstgirls.com
Tech Ladies: hiretechladies.com
Inclusion Geeks: inclusiongeeks.com
Elephant in the Valley: elephantinthevalley.com
Fairygodboss: fairygodboss.com
Rewriting the Code: rewritingthecode.org
Women in Tech: women-in-tech.org
Women in Technology (WIT): mywit.org
American Association of University Women: aauw.org
Association for Women in Science (AWIS): awis.org
Society of STEM Women of Color (SSWOC): sswoc.org

Acknowledgments

Wow—first of all, thank you for reading this book! And if you're reading the acknowledgments—that's a double high five for sure. I'm a not-famous person, and this is my first published book, so you really had no way of knowing if it would be worth your time. Thank you for reading, and I hope you enjoyed it.

Thank you to my agent, Chip Rice at WordLink, who also took a chance on this not-famous person. I feel very secure knowing you represent my writing. Hopefully there's more to come!

Thanks also to Karen Boss, my editor at Charlesbridge, who helped me polish this story to be much better than it originally was, and who ultimately put Cam's story in your hands.

To my friends who helped along the way: Stefy Cohen for answering my questions about Spanish and Panamanian culture, and Kim Conner for the headshots that make me look so legit.

Thank you to Jackie Dever, for a lovely and astute copyedit. To Oriol Vidal, whose cover illustration made Cam real. To Diane Earley, the creative director at Charlesbridge for her excellent design. To Esther Reisberg for the thorough proofread. And to the entire team at Charlesbridge for all their work to sell and market this story.

The hugest, biggest thank-you to my husband and partner, Kevin, who had to do a lot of extra childcare so I could revise this book for publication, and who continues to do more childcare so I can keep writing while we both also work full-time jobs with a toddler (read: agent of chaos) in our house. I know our son is fun and cute, but so is napping and having personal time. I see and appreciate your sacrifice, Kevin. I love you.

And of course, thank you to Oliver for being so fun and cute. I hope you read this one day and are 100 percent not like the guys who make Cam's life hard. I think you're already on the right track. Sorry for the curse words. Or not. Cursing is fine, actually, in the right context. Mama loves you.